D1544757

DEATH AMID GEMS

Other books by Meagan J. Meehan:

Dry Heat

DEATH AMID GEMS

•

Meagan J. Meehan

AVALON BOOKS
NEW YORK

© 2011 by Meagan J. Meehan
All rights reserved.
All the characters in this book are fictitious,
and any resemblance to actual persons,
living or dead, is purely coincidental.
Published by Avalon Books,
an imprint of Thomas Bouregy & Co., Inc.
160 Madison Avenue, New York, NY 10016

Library of Congress Cataloging-in-Publication Data

Meehan, Meagan J.
   Death amid gems / Meagan J. Meehan.
      p. cm.
   ISBN 978-0-8034-7654-7 (acid-free paper) 1. Young women—
Crimes against—Fiction.   2. Murder—Investigation—Fiction.
3. Police—New York (State)—Long Island—Fiction.
4. Jewelry trade—Fiction.   5. Home shopping television
programs—Fiction.   6. Christmas decorations—Fiction.
7. Nephews—Fiction.   8. Long Island (N.Y.)—Fiction.
I. Title.
PS3613.E368D43 2011
813'.6—dc22

                                                    2010037165

PRINTED IN THE UNITED STATES OF AMERICA
ON ACID-FREE PAPER
BY RR DONNELLEY, BLOOMSBURG, PENNSYLVANIA

155494

419

tax

11
4/

To my wonderful parents, Michael and Mary,
and to my friend Chris, the detective-in-training

Chapter One

Beneath the glare of the bright halogen lights, the spilled gems sparkled furiously. There were dozens of small shiny jewels littered across the floor in an astonishing array of color. Red rubies, green emeralds, purple amethysts, blue sapphires, and every type and shade in between lay on the off-white tiles like tiny islands engulfed within a sea of blood. A few inches away from them lay the still body of a young woman, her blue eyes open in a permanent state of surprise. Aside from the hum of the overhead lights, the room was silent.

The clanking of keys disrupted the stillness in the air as the janitor, a young man of Latin origin, walked into the room, weary after a bad night of sleep followed by an early start at work. He was used to dull mornings on the job where he was required to sweep the floor and empty the trash cans. He was not accustomed to seeing blood and bodies. When he saw the dead woman, he screamed, turned, and ran to get help as fast as his legs would carry him.

The shrill ring of the phone awoke Detective Angelo Zenoni from his dreams of Caribbean beaches, tropical fish, and warm weather, bringing him back to the chilly New York climate. Although it was only November, the weather was unusually cold and icy. Zenoni reached for the phone on his bedside table without removing himself from under the covers. He could hear the wind whipping against the windows, howling like a wolf. *So much for global warming,* he thought sarcastically as he voiced a gruff and sleepy "hello" into the phone.

"Morning, Angelo," the voice on the other end declared, making the detective groan mentally. He recognized the voice immediately as Lieutenant Bob Rudd, who would only call if there were a full-blown emergency underway.

"What's happening, Bob?" Zenoni asked, stealing a glance at his bedside clock: 6:43 in the morning, too early to deal with police work.

"We've got a murder. I just got off the phone with Sergeant Veglak; a woman's dead at a television studio over in Eastwood. He says you need to get over there ASAP."

"Tell him I'll be there in a half hour."

"Will do. I had a heck of a time reaching you; the cell's not working."

"That's because I shut it off at night to prevent work calls when I'm off duty and trying to sleep," Zenoni replied, rubbing his sleepy eyes. "Are you going to call Wildow?" he added, suddenly thinking of his partner.

"I already did. He's always easier to get ahold of than you."

"Yeah, yeah. I'll see you later, Bob."

Yawning, Zenoni placed the phone back in its cradle and looked over at Lorraine, his wife of twenty-eight years, who was sleeping peacefully beside him. As usual, she had slept through the phone ringing and his conversation. *I shoulda been an author,* he thought forlornly as he untangled himself from the bedsheets.

He showered and dressed before making his way to the kitchen for a quick breakfast. Navigating around the room wasn't easy. Paints and colored pencils were scattered about, so much so that it resembled an art supply obstacle course. Lorraine, a children's book author, often worked on illustrations for her books at the kitchen table. Zenoni wasn't exactly sure what the latest story was about, but he knew it involved talking penguins building igloos. *It looks pretty good so far,* he thought as he prepared his coffee. Lorraine had already informed him that, as always, he was to read and review the story for her before she sent it in to the publisher and, although he would be pressed to admit it, he was looking forward to the task.

A nudge at his calf followed by a soft "meow" roused him from his thoughts. Napoleon, their gray and white tabby, was demanding his breakfast.

"Right on schedule; you never change," Zenoni remarked as he grappled with a can of cat food. As soon as the aroma of the tuna and gravy feast filled the air, Napoleon purred and swished his tail, and Zenoni's stomach lurched. Thanksgiving had been on Thursday and even now, five days later, his stomach had not yet fully recovered from dinner at the home of his sister-in-law, Denise. Lorraine was close to her only sibling and she wouldn't even consider turning down the invitation despite the fact that Denise was a notoriously bad cook. Years of police work had left Zenoni with more than one ulcer, which added to his pain. He often thought if he hadn't left the city and transferred closer to his Long Island home, his nerves would be frayed to nothing by now. He liked his Long Island post but, at fifty-five years of age, with thirty-two years on the force, retirement was becoming more and more appealing.

He had hoped to be out of the house before Lorraine awoke, but as he searched through the coin dish on the living room shelf for his car keys, she appeared in the doorway. By nature she was not an early riser. Her dark shoulder-length hair was askew, her green eyes puffy with sleep, and the morning sun exposed every wrinkle on her face. Rarely did she look so disheveled.

"You're up early," she mused through a yawn.

"I got a call. Don't worry about it. Go back to bed."

"I assure you, I will," Lorraine replied sleepily, as she made her way toward the kitchen. "I was thinking, on your way home tonight, why don't you stop by the storage warehouse and pick up some of the Christmas stuff?"

"Don't bother me about that now, please."

"I don't mean to, but it's after Thanksgiving, and you wouldn't do it over the weekend—"

"That's because I'm still recovering from Denise's dinner disaster."

Lorraine looked up from the contents of the fridge and glared at Zenoni in what he assumed was supposed to be a warning look. She was not, however, able to hide a slight smile at the corner of her mouth.

"That's not nice. Denise worked hard on that dinner and it was sweet of her to invite us. Seriously though, don't change the subject. I don't want to nag you, but the Christmas season is upon us and these decorations take a long time to set up; you know that as well as I do."

"All right already, I'll deal with the decorations at some point. I just don't want to think about them right now. It's early, my stomach is sore, and I think I'm about to go see a dead body, so I have more on my mind than Rudolph the Red-Nosed Reindeer."

Lorraine was in the process of pouring herself a glass of orange juice when she heard the word *body*. Immediately she put down the carton of juice, leaving the glass half-filled, and looked at her husband with concern.

"Be careful, Angelo, okay? You know I worry about you dealing with these things."

"I know," he replied, planting a kiss on his wife's cheek, "but I always come back safe, right? So just relax, and as we decorate the tree, we'll talk about retirement plans."

With that said, he left the house, got into the black Chevy Impala he used as a police car, turned on the flashing lights, and headed toward his case.

When he first arrived at the murder scene, Detective Zenoni felt as if he had entered into some kind of chaotic outdoor opera. News vans and police vehicles were everywhere. A large group of onlookers were being held back as another group holding signs—clearly protesters—shouted hostile remarks at the officers. Looming on the right side of the driveway entrance, a large sign informed visitors that they had reached THE TREAS-URE CHEST JEWELRY TELEVISION STUDIO.

Eastwood was a wide stretch of land inhabited by offices of all shapes and sizes. Some of the businesses in the area—such as the banks—were housed in modern buildings with multi-million dollar budgets, while warehouse stores were simply tacked onto the strip as convenient locations for suburbanites to pick up groceries. The Treasure Chest Jewelry Television Studio, in between the ritz and the rubble, wasn't open to the general public, but one glance at its somewhat shabby appearance made it clear that the company was not immune to bud-get problems. After showing his badge, Zenoni parked his car toward the back of the lot to avoid onlookers and pushy reporters. The commotion outside the studio had brought a considerable number of early-morning commuters together to gawk.

Almost as soon as he was out of his car, his partner, Nolan Wildow, was beside him. Although he was only in his early forties, Wildow's hair was graying and balding. He was a small and slight man whose hazel eyes appeared large and owlish behind thick glasses. For the past five years, Wildow and Zenoni had been partners, and they got along well despite their differences. Wildow paid attention to the slightest of details when involved in a case and he had the keenest observation skills Zenoni had ever seen. He could also be a hard-nosed interrogator if need be, a trait that belied both his appearance and his personal background. Wildow was the son of an overly protective mother and he had married an equally controlling woman. Work was his one salvation from constant nagging and he took his job seriously.

"Crazy out here, huh?" Wildow declared as soon as he was within Zenoni's earshot.

"Sure is. The news got hold of this one fast."

"The studio is only a block away."

"How long have you been here?"

Wildow glanced at his watch. "About twenty minutes. Unlike some people, I'm an early riser."

"Yeah, yeah. So what've we got so far?"

Wildow looked down at his leather-encased notepad. "The victim was Tiffany Kehl: twenty-six and a studio employee. Her car is parked near the back entrance of this place. We have it roped off. That's all we've got as of now. We've rounded up her colleagues from other parts of the building to shield them from the media circus as they wait to be interviewed. We've already had trouble with one of the cameramen. He kept trying to come out here and blab to the news crews so he could be on TV."

"Who found the body?" Zenoni asked, as he eyed a young patrol officer desperately attempting to control a growing crowd of pedestrians.

Wildow shifted his notes. "Luis Morales, age twenty-nine. He's a janitor who works in the building. He doesn't speak much English, so we got a patrol officer, Eddie Garcia, who's going to translate for him. The story is that, first thing this morning, Luis walked into the back room to clean out the garbage cans and saw the body. It's a mess in there and the sight of it sent him running for the door. What's strange is that the nine-one-one call came from the gas station across the street. That's also where Luis was when the first patrol officers arrived."

"It's bad on the scene?"

"I haven't seen it yet, but forensics eyeballed the place and said there's a fair bit of blood."

Zenoni felt his already queasy stomach plummet once again; he didn't like the sight of blood. Grisly scenes gave him nightmares.

"And one other thing," Wildow declared, somewhat reluctantly. "I've been told there's a problem with some of the security cameras, so there's a good chance nothing was caught on tape."

"Great. Just perfect," Zenoni spat sarcastically. The absence of security cameras was going to make things more difficult. "What's with the picket sign group?"

"They're some sort of anti-corporation, pro-humanity group protesting what they call *blood gems*."

"How long have they been here?"

"According to the station manager, about three weeks."

"Where's the manager now?"

"He's inside awaiting an interview, like lots of others."

Zenoni nodded; a plan was already forming inside his head. "Okay, we'll go take a look at the crime scene and the body, and then check out the car to see if there's any kind of evidence in there. Then we'll go and talk to this Morales guy. Have the protesters rounded up and get their names. I want to speak to the leaders even before I speak to the studio employees."

During his years as a law enforcement agent, Zenoni had seen his share of bodies and blood. His black hair had turned gray, his smooth face had wrinkled, and his toned body had rounded from the constant shock and stress of various cases. Yet, despite his lengthy experience, he found the scene inside the jewelry studio unusually brutal. The young woman lying on the floor had been bludgeoned to death with such force that part of her head had caved in. Her blue eyes were still open, vacantly staring into nothing. Small unmounted gems sparkled furiously on all sides of her like confetti. An empty plastic carrying tray, meant for transporting jewels, lay about three feet away from the body, and inches from that lay a bloody unplugged lamp. Its black extension cord sat on the floor like a dead snake. The only other furniture in the station's back room was a large wooden desk, an ancient office chair, and a number of metal file cabinets with locks on them.

Tiffany Kehl had been pretty, even if it wasn't an entirely natural sort of pretty. She was small framed and around five foot six. Her hair was blond with brown roots and her acrylic nails were perfectly manicured into a style Zenoni had heard Lorraine call "French tips." Her light skin was covered in makeup, and her fingers, ears, neck, and wrists were dotted with gold-encased jewels—all pink sapphires to match the pink designer blouse she was wearing. Zenoni also noted that, although her pants were black, her expensive-looking shoes and handbag matched the shade of her top perfectly. This was a woman who held style in high regard. The most personal touch was the chain on the keys Tiffany held tightly in her hand. It contained a picture of a small, reddish-brown dog. Zenoni recognized the breed as Pomeranian.

"She practiced what she preached," Wildow commented. "She liked jewelry, and since none was taken from her, I doubt this was a run-of-the-mill robbery gone bad. It looks like it happened a few hours ago, though, probably in the middle of the night. She's been dead a while; the body's cold."

Zenoni nodded in agreement. "No wedding ring, so we can assume she wasn't married. Obviously she was holding the tray when she fell and that's what caused the gems to spill. It looks like she was hit from behind. Was the door forced?"

"No. Bill checked it out this morning and the lock is intact. Whoever did this was either allowed in or the door was unlocked."

Zenoni nodded. Bill Everson was the forensics specialist. He surveyed his scenes carefully and wouldn't pass on information unless he knew it was absolutely accurate.

"Any fingerprints?"

"Not that he's seen so far, but he's waiting for us to take a look in here before he checks the lamp that, I think it's safe to say, looks like our murder weapon."

"My guess is that the killer was probably wearing gloves," Zenoni announced, squatting down to get a better look at the body. "It's been cold out, so lack of fingerprint evidence isn't all that surprising. It seems like she knew whoever did this; there's no sign of a struggle. She's holding car keys, so maybe she was about to leave for the night when someone confronted her. Maybe they were having a fight and she turned her back for just second and *whack*! I suppose the lamp was sitting right on the desk and it was the first thing the killer could grab. This girl was hit more than once, that's obvious. Whatever else this was about, the murder was done in a fit of rage."

"The question is, over what?" Wildow remarked.

"That's it exactly," Zenoni replied, as he picked up and unzipped Tiffany's pocketbook. Wildow came closer to investigate the contents with his partner. There were a few sets of keys, a small silver cell phone, a small container of tissues, a makeup bag, and a ladies' wallet. Zenoni opened the wallet and discovered Tiffany's license and address, cash, credit cards, checkbook and many photos of the dog on the keychain. Carefully, he fished her second set of car keys out of the purse and turned to his partner.

"There's nothing out of the ordinary in the pocketbook. Let's just go make sure the car is clean and then we'll start asking questions."

The day had gotten a little brighter, but it was still quite cold when Zenoni and Wildow walked out to the parking lot to investigate Tiffany's car. It was a shiny recent-year Toyota Solaris—a red convertible. Zenoni wasn't exactly surprised when he saw that the car had been loaded with luxury extras like a GPS system and heated leather front seats. The car was neat and tidy. There were lotto tickets and dry cleaning orders in the glove compartment and takeout menus from various restaurants in the side compartment of the door—nothing out of place. The trunk was more interesting: a number of blankets and warm ladies' coats were sprawled within the space, alongside cans of food and bottled water.

"What do you suppose this was all about?" Wildow asked, staring at the strange contents of the trunk.

"I have no idea, but it's weird," Zenoni replied. "Make sure pictures are taken of this. We're going to have a lot of piecing together to do over the next few days."

Wildow nodded. "Let's go interview the janitor who found the body. Hopefully he'll be able to tell us something about the victim."

Zenoni wasted no time in making his way back toward the warm studio; staying outside in such cold weather was a good way to catch the flu, and given how busy he felt he was going to get within the next few days, his health was not something he could afford to risk.

Luis Morales was visibly shaken. He sat on the couch in the janitor break room, surrounded by uniformed police officers, twiddling his thumbs nervously. He jumped in surprise at the sound of the door opening as Zenoni and Wildow entered the room.

The poor guy looks scared half to death, Zenoni thought, while observing the bleak break room. The tiny space was painted the same dismal gray as Luis' janitor uniform; there were no windows or pictures. The only furniture in the room was a worn blue couch and a rickety wooden coffee table. In the corner, a small-screen television sat on an old stand beside an ancient vending machine.

"Luis Morales, I'm Detective Wildow." Wildow began holding his hand out. Luis looked at him somewhat distrustfully before tentatively shaking his hand.

"And I'm Detective Zenoni," Zenoni added, also offering to shake hands. "Can you tell us what happened here this morning?"

"He speaks only Spanish, so I need to translate for him," Officer Garcia explained as Luis looked helplessly from one police officer to the other.

"Go ahead," Wildow replied.

The detective's questions were translated to Luis, who replied immediately in a quivering voice that matched the trembling of his body.

"He says he came to sweep the floor and saw her lying there. He's pretty shaken. He says the only other dead body he's ever seen was at his grandmother's funeral and he's never seen this much blood anywhere."

"Ask him if he saw anyone else around."

Luis said he hadn't.

"Our reports indicate that the nine-one-one call came from the gas station across the street. Why did he go there? Why not make the call from here?"

Garcia turned and questioned Luis, whose face was a mask of stress. He stared mostly at the floor, but raised his eyes just enough to give the two detectives conspicuous glances. Although he seemed nervous—actually, downright afraid—he answered the questions without hesitation. He spoke for a long time before rapidly speeding up and accompanying his speech with elaborate hand gestures. Garcia looked at the detectives once Luis was silent.

"He says he panicked when he saw the blood, and his mind went blank. He has a friend over at the gas station that speaks better English. He thought the operator would understand his friend easier."

Zenoni nodded. That made sense.

"There's one other thing," Garcia continued cautiously.

"What's that?"

"He's illegal," Garcia explained, gesturing toward the janitor. "He's terrified of being deported."

"Tell him that we are dealing with a murder investigation, and he did not do anything wrong, so there's no reason to worry," Wildow replied.

Garcia passed the message along to Luis.

"Ask him if he knew the dead girl," Zenoni ordered, pleased to see that Luis was now visibly more relaxed and comfortable enough to look at him directly. "If he did know her, what was she like?"

"He says he knew her a little, not personally, but he saw her around while he was working. Her name was Tiffany and she was one of the sales girls who appeared on television. He says aside from the occasional 'hello,' or 'clean that up,' she never paid much attention to him."

"Does he know of anyone she was having trouble with? Did he ever see her arguing with anyone here or on the phone?"

Garcia translated the questions. This time Luis didn't answer immediately. He looked from one law enforcement agent to another with a worried expression, sighed, and replied.

"He says that she argued on her cell phone a lot, but he has no idea with whom. She was also unhappy about the protesters outside; apparently they egged her car one day. He also says—and he's afraid of losing his job for this—that he saw her and the station manager fighting in the hallway last week; it was a pretty bad argument."

"What's the manager's name?" Wildow demanded. Although Garcia translated the question, Luis answered clearly enough for everyone to understand—Arnold Genson—before adding another line in Spanish.

"What was that last bit?"

"He says Genson is probably here now. He comes to work around the same time the janitors do."

"Okay, we'll get to questioning everyone else in a little while," Zenoni explained. "As of now is there anything else that he can think to tell us?"

Garcia asked and Luis wearily shook his head.

"Okay then," Zenoni replied, "tell him to go home and get some rest. He looks like he needs to take it easy. Tell him we thank him for his time and he's been very helpful."

The janitor slouched gratefully in his chair, glad to be over with the questioning. As he left the room, escorted by Officer Garcia, Wildow turned to Zenoni.

"I think he's telling the truth."

"Me too. The guy's shaking like a leaf in the breeze. My gut tells me he had nothing to do with this, aside from finding the body, but someone else here might have. Let's get on with the interviewing. I'll go outside and deal with the protesters. You go talk to the station manager."

"On my way," Wildow replied, turning to leave the room. Zenoni followed, shutting the employee break room door behind him. It squeaked like a frightened mouse. As he made his way out toward the cold, he sighed. He had a feeling this was going to be a very tiring and complex case.

Chapter Two

The chill in the air outside the studio was biting. It nipped at Zenoni's ears, making him wish he had a pair of earmuffs handy. His one comfort was the wool gloves he wore, saving his fingers from frostbite as he took notes.

The protesters, flanked by police officers, were dressed to withstand the weather. Their multilayered attire made Zenoni think of a Christmas song line, *". . . bundled up like Eskimos."* He shook the thought from his mind quickly. Christmas was one thing he couldn't think about while he was investigating a murder. Despite the morning's chaos, the protesters were still picketing and shouting at the surrounding officers. Angelo approached the group displaying his badge.

"I'm Detective Zenoni. Who's in charge here?"

"We're all doing our part to stop what the jewelry industry is doing to this world," a plump woman with frizzy red hair retorted. She held a sign requesting readers to KEEP GEMS UNDERGROUND.

"That's great," the detective replied, with a deadpan look on his face. "I'm inquiring about a murder. I will ask you again, who's in charge of this group?"

"If you have to know, my husband and me," the woman said as a tall middle-aged man with wild gray hair approached her.

"Is there a problem here?" he asked, as he placed a protective hand on his wife's shoulder.

"I'm Detective Zenoni," Angelo declared once again, flashing his badge. "I'm investigating a murder that took place here this morning. I have reports that indicate your group has been on this property for a number of weeks and—"

"It's ironic that you're investigating a murder here, a place that supports the enslavement of thousands of people worldwide!" the gray-haired man spat out angrily, color rising in his cheeks.

"Uh-huh," Angelo replied nonchalantly. "Might I have your name, sir?" he asked, flipping his black leather-bound notebook to a clean page.

"Otto Simic. And don't think you'll stop our cause by pegging us as troublemakers. This has been a peaceful protest through and through! We stand out here every day from six in the morning to nine at night, and there's been no police called until now—and this has nothing to do with us!"

"I never said it did. Now what's your name?" the detective queried, turning to the plump woman.

"Hazel Simic," she said, "and I stand by my husband's words. You won't stop this protest until you stop the distribution of blood gems!"

"Do you have any idea of the results of this industry?" Otto asked dramatically, pointing toward the jewelry studio. "Financing of warlord activities, enslavement, torture, death—all a result of the products this establishment offers!"

"I'm not here to discuss world affairs. I'm here to ask some questions related to a murder investigation. Did any of you know Tiffany Kehl?"

"We don't know the names of any of *those* people," Hazel sneered.

"So, you've been out here daily for close to a month and you don't even know the names of the people you're protesting against?"

"Well, we're not protesting the people!" Otto snapped.

"We're protesting the industry and the practices it allows. We don't deal with the studio employees at all. They wouldn't even let us in to show them photos of the victims they've created."

"You're honestly telling me, after all the hours you've spent standing out here, you wouldn't recognize anyone from the building?"

"Not by name . . . but by sight maybe," Hazel offered, somewhat reluctantly. "Can you give a description?"

Relieved to have someone cooperate, Angelo flipped a few notebook pages back and read the description. "Tiffany Kehl, age twenty-six. She was about five feet six and one hundred and thirty pounds, Caucasian, blond hair, blue eyes."

"Oh yes, *her*," Hazel hissed. "I know who you're talking about. She was the one who wore all the jewelry and makeup and the high heels, right?"

Angelo nodded.

"Well, she was just the rudest woman! The exact type I'd expect to see selling blood diamonds! Every time she saw us, she gave us dirty looks. Once Otto called out to her, asking her to save herself and repent for her sinful job. She answered him in less-than-ladylike terms. She had a red convertible and she drove like a lunatic, no regard for the law whatsoever. Tiffany was her name, was it? I've never liked that name."

"Well, from what I was told, she had reason to shoot you dirty looks. Apparently one time she came out of work and found her car egged, and it had been parked right near you guys. It sounds like she started parking and entering the studio from the back lot to avoid further confrontation."

"There's no proof of any of that," Hazel scoffed.

"Mr. and Mrs. Simic, where were you last night?" Angelo asked, his pen poised to take notes.

"How dare you!" Hazel screeched. "We are supporters of peace. We would never murder someone, not even her!"

"It's just procedure, ma'am. I need to know where you and your husband were last night since the victim had experienced incidents involving you."

"Allegedly!" Hazel hissed before adding, "There's seventeen of us in this group, and we were all together last night."

Angelo raised his eyebrows in disbelief.

"It's true," Otto explained. "We're a group of people with a united interest in improving the world, but we don't all live close to one another. We started our little club online. Some of these people have come all the way from Canada to be here. So, since we're all fighting for the same cause, my wife and I figured we'd all stay at the same hotel for as long as this thing lasts."

"Which hotel?" Angelo asked, skeptical.

"The Hammock. It's a little place right off Route 10."

"And all of you have been there since this protest began three weeks ago?"

"Three and a half weeks actually, but yes," Otto replied.

Angelo shook his head. "Must be quite a bill."

"That's not an issue, considering the cause."

"And you're sure you know nothing else about the dead girl?"

"No. I told you, we never went near the workers or the building after the first time they put us out. The reason we stand on the sidewalk here is because it's public property and they can't ask us to move. I know my rights."

Zenoni nodded. He reckoned that these folks would be well aware of how to legally defend themselves during clashes with the law. For the next few minutes, he collected the names and addresses of the protest group members. If it was true that they were all accounted for in one hotel the previous evening, it would save some time and be a stroke of luck in his career.

Arnold Genson was nervous. That fact would have been apparent to anyone who saw him in his cramped, messy office.

Arnold's pudgy hands were shaking, his round face drained of color, and sweat was dripping from him as if from a leaking faucet as he sat facing Nolan Wildow. Wildow expected the manager of a mid-sized studio like this to handle stress better and thought the display of nerves unusual. Then again, people reacted differently in situations where a dead body was involved.

"I can't believe it," Arnold stammered, ringing his hands together.

"Better start," Wildow replied casually. "Tiffany's dead and a source tells me that you were seen arguing with her shortly before her death. Is that true?"

"Who said that?" Arnold snapped, showing a flash of anger so intense that Wildow momentarily feared being punched.

"I told you, a source."

"Which source? I'd be careful believing people around here. They like to point fingers, especially at me, since I'm the one who has to run this place. It's not easy, I'll tell you that."

"It seems I struck a nerve," Wildow continued, playing into the manager's temper. "Suddenly you're very willing to talk to me."

"I'll defend myself when I need to."

"Why do you need to? What is it these people say about you?"

"It's just a tough job, okay? And if something, I mean *anything*, goes wrong, it's automatically my fault. It grates on my nerves."

"How about Tiffany? Did she grate on your nerves?"

Arnold's light blue eyes fixed Wildow with a cold stare. "Yeah, I'm not going to lie. She was one of the worst complainers in this place. If she wasn't a top earner, I would have had her sacked years ago."

"So you didn't get along with her?"

"No, not really. I tried, but she was impossible to deal with. She never minded her own business, and she was always on my case about something. Work was her life; she was here all the time."

"Why was she giving you such a hard time?"

"Her main complaint was that I didn't manage things right. How's that for nerve? She had no idea how much work I did, but whenever one item got misplaced or one inventory sheet went missing, she would come after me yelling and screaming. She actually used to come looking for me. Once she waited outside the men's room. Crazy, huh?"

"So what was the last argument you had with her about?"

"She was criticizing my time management skills. She said that I wasn't around enough to know what was happening. She couldn't find one of the gem cases and she thought I should have been supervising the inventory more carefully."

"I heard it got pretty heated."

"Well, she was threatening my job. She said she'd go to the CEO in California if push came to shove. I believed her too. She scared me. I need this job. I spent years trying to get it."

"So, naturally, you'd be pretty upset if someone tried to take it from you."

"Sure. But that doesn't mean I killed her."

"Where were you last night, Mr. Genson?"

"Why do you want to know?"

"It's standard procedure. Please answer the question."

"I was bowling."

"Which alley?"

"Lucky Lanes, over in Quailbrooke."

"And you were there all night?"

"Pretty much. I'm an insomniac and the place is open twenty-four hours. I guess I left around one in the morning, maybe two."

"And then?"

"I went home."

"Did you stop anywhere?"

"No. I didn't kill her."

An uneasy silence passed between the men for a few moments before Nolan Wildow continued his questioning.

"What do you know about Tiffany personally?"

"Not much. Trust me, we didn't spend time together unless we had to."

"Do you know of any family or friends she had?"

"As I said, I didn't know her well, but I don't think she was married. I really don't know though."

Wildow nodded and closed his notepad. "Okay, Mr. Genson, you're free to go, but don't plan on taking any trips. We might need to speak with you again as the investigation progresses."

Although he had only been in the room with him for under a minute, Angelo already disliked the sloppy man in the gray uniform waiting to be questioned. They were back in the janitors' break room, and the man was Hector Harte, the other custodian employed on the premises.

"Mr. Harte, I'm Detective Zenoni. I'm here to ask you some questions about a murder that took place here late last night or in the early hours of this morning."

"I don't know nothing," Hector retorted, leaning back into his chair nonchalantly.

Angelo examined the individual before him. Harte was in his early forties, but looked younger. His bluish-gray janitor's jumpsuit, sagging off his scrawny frame, was covered in stains. His lax brown hair was greasy, accompanied by a pronounced five o'clock shadow spread across the lower half of his face. He was a shady-looking character—the type that might be seen spending his weekly wages at the racetrack or in a bar. He had a listlessness about him that was both off-putting and yet expected by his appearance.

"Did you work last night, Hector?"

"Yeah, until eleven-thirty."

"You're here early again today."

"I'm working extra hours. My schedule always gets hectic around this time of year but, hey, it's good to have some of that overtime dough. You know what I mean?"

"How many hours do you work?"

"I'm scheduled for nights, so my time is usually from four-thirty in the afternoon to eleven-thirty at night, but until the Christmas season ends, it's three-thirty until midnight. Around the holidays, the sales start, and more boxes of jewels come in. Once the cases are open, it's up to me and Luis to clean up the discarded packages. Sometimes we're forced to work overtime. I've been stuck here until three in the morning some nights."

"Long hours, one way or another."

Hector shrugged. "It's a living, and I got weekends off."

Angelo nodded and cut to the chase. "Tiffany Kehl—did you know her?"

"Yeah: tall blond, usually had a sour look on her face. Is she the one who got whacked?"

"I'm afraid so. It doesn't sound like you two got along well."

Hector shrugged and leaned further back against the wall. He was trying to play it as if he was relaxed, but Angelo had been on enough cases to recognize the signs of someone who knew something he didn't want to say.

"I'll remind you that this is a murder investigation, Mr. Harte. I would not suggest withholding evidence. Now, what do you know about Tiffany Kehl?" The sharp tone of the lawman's voice made Hector look up and glare at him disdainfully.

"I'm a janitor. What do you expect me to know? I saw her

occasionally, just passing glances in the hallway mostly. I'll admit that she wasn't bad to look at, but she was always ticked off about something. Besides, I got a woman."

"I never said you didn't. So, Tiffany had a temper. What made her angry?"

"Everything. Anything. She screamed at me once because a lightbulb blew out and, according to her, I didn't change it fast enough."

"Pretty harsh. When was the last time you saw her?"

"Right before I went home last night. She was in the back room, going through some paperwork and talking to herself. I said good night, but I don't think she even heard me. Then I got in my truck and drove home to Oakwood. I got in around one in the morning. You can ask my woman."

"Oakwood is a long way away."

"It's not bad. I don't mind driving as long as I got my radio tuned to the country station."

"So you heard and saw nothing strange last night and went straight home after leaving here?"

"Yup."

"Okay. Do you know anything about her family or friends?"

"I know she hung around with some of the other girls here. I bet a number of them are outside right now, but I'm not sure since the cops insisted on keeping all of us separated."

"Do you know the names of the other girls Tiffany spent time with?"

"Julie and Amy, and one more . . . Betty or something."

"Last names?"

"How should I know?"

"Records indicate you've worked here four years."

"Yeah and I mind my own business. Unless you stay to yourself around here, people jump all over you. There's always somebody trying to find some way to make you work harder than you got to."

"Okay, Mr. Harte, thank you for your time," Angelo announced, closing his notebook and locking eyes with the rough-looking janitor. "We'll be back to speak with you if anything comes up."

Nolan Wildow was a curt, straight-to-the-point, emotionally detached interviewer, yet with Amy Kennedy, he knew he would have to be more sympathetic. She was young, maybe twenty-three, and obviously distraught over Tiffany's death. Her freckled face was white with shock and her blue eyes damp with tears. Her long red hair hung over her small frame, which shook every time she let out a sob. She was being interviewed in the employee break room; it resembled the janitor's room, except with a newer couch, a bigger television, a small window, and a few plants.

"I can't believe it," she uttered for what must have been the hundredth time. "Really? I mean, she's gone? I worked beside her for three years and now . . . I can't believe it."

"Did you know Tiffany well?"

Amy nodded. "Yeah. Well, sorta. She was hard to read sometimes. We worked shows together pretty often, and we usually had lunch at least once a week. She was really good at her job. I mean, she was amazing. She knew exactly what she wanted and how to get it. She talked about having her own company one day—with a personal magazine and a show. She loved her work. That's one of the reasons I spent so much time with her. I figured I could learn a few things and she could be really nice. She never let me pay for lunch, not ever, even if I insisted. I'm the youngest girl here, so she kinda took me under her wing."

"So at lunch you talked about work?"

"Mostly. That was Tiffany's favorite topic, aside from her dog."

Wildow nodded, remembering the keychain with the photo of the Pomeranian on it. "Can you think of anyone who may have wanted to hurt her?"

Amy shook her head. "No one."

"Do you know of any family or friends?"

"As I said, we didn't talk that much about personal stuff, but I do know that she was fairly close to her parents. Well, as close as Tiffany got to anyone."

"Okay, tell me about her parents."

"I don't know them personally, but Tiffany told me a little. Her dad's retired; I think he was a foot doctor or something—"

"A podiatrist?"

"Yeah, that's it. I think his name's Thomas, Tom for short. Her mother is Evelyn, Eve. I know that since she was always calling Tiffany. If her mother was at a supermarket or something, she would call just to make absolutely sure Tiffany didn't need anything. They were concerned like that, you know?"

"How did Tiffany react to the calls?"

"She'd seem kinda annoyed, because she was really self-sufficient, but she also seemed somewhat grateful. I know she saw her parents a few times a week. They live in Melvin Field, down Woolington Avenue."

Good, that's not too far from here, Wildow thought, flashing Amy a reassuring smile as he scribbled notes. "How about boyfriends? Do you know if Tiffany had one?"

Amy blushed slightly. "Tiffany was kind of a tease. She wasn't really into steady relationships. I think she was seeing someone, but I don't know who he was or even what his name was."

"How do you know about him then?"

"I was with her at lunch one day when he called. She was talking in this teasing voice she used when she was speaking to men she liked."

Wildow nodded as he completed his notes. He then turned a kind eye to Amy, who was still struggling to compose herself. "You've been extremely helpful to the investigation, Miss Kennedy. Thank you very much."

Amy forced a smile. "It's no problem. I only wish I knew more."

"Well, what you do know is going to come in handy," he replied sincerely.

As soon as Amy was out of his sight, Wildow radioed into headquarters, requesting the exact address of the Kehls. He expected that he would be meeting with them within the next few hours.

Bridget Sutton, a plus-size girl in her late twenties, sat on the old gray stool inside the studio's financial records room looking absolutely bewildered. She wore too much makeup, yet her dark eyes and thick raven hair were undeniably attractive. Bridget wasn't exactly what most men considered "hot," so Zenoni wasn't surprised that Hector had been unable to remember her name.

"She's dead?" Bridget asked, staring at Zenoni with disbelieving eyes.

The detective nodded. "I'm afraid so. Were you close to her?"

"I had lunch with her a few times, but we didn't see each other much since I don't do shows. I'm just a receptionist. She was superambitious though. Her temper was quick, but she was excellent at her job."

"Did you ever talk to her about nonwork-related topics?"

Bridget shook her head. "Not really. Work was Tiffany's life. I know she was finishing up her master's in business at Holson University. It's a few miles away from here; she used to go directly from work on Wednesday nights."

"Did she like school?"

"She liked the idea of getting her MBA. She thought it would be a big step to propelling her career forward. She said some of the teachers knew less than she did, but Tiffany was kind of arrogant."

"Did she have trouble with her professors?"

"Nothing serious, although I heard her say she exchanged words with this Professor Mathis guy. However, she did have real trouble with another student. Tiffany said some crazed classmate accused her of trying to steal her boyfriend. The girl keyed her car; she just got it fixed about a week ago."

"Did she mention any names?"

"I think the name was Olivia, but I'm not sure."

"Okay, and you have no idea who might have wanted to do this?"

Bridget shook her head vigorously. "No. Tiffany could be demanding and self-centered, but I really can't imagine anyone wanting to kill her."

"Okay then, thank you for your time. You've been very helpful. If I have any further questions, I'll contact you."

"Sure," Bridget replied. "I hope you catch whoever did this."

So do I, Zenoni thought. This was turning out to be a very complicated case.

Julianna Armas was shocked and distressed by the news of Tiffany's death. She stared at Nolan Wildow as if he was some sort of exotic animal, as she breathlessly questioned him about the rumors she'd heard of the death. The detective allowed

Julianna a few moments to let the shock of the confirmation sink in before he started to question her. Once again, the interview was being conducted in the employee break room.

"Did you know her well?"

Julianna nodded. "Yeah, we were pretty cool with each other. She was intense with her job, but she could also be really fun to hang out with. When we were off work, we'd go to clubs and stuff."

"What was she like on those occasions?"

"She was fun. We had stuff in common, so we were really able to connect."

"What kind of stuff?"

"Our jobs and our sense of humor—things like that. We both liked to check out the latest fashion trends too; Tiffany thought that looking good was a big part of being successful."

"When you were at these clubs, was there any drug or alcohol use?"

Julianna looked outraged. "Absolutely not! I'd have a few glasses of champagne, but nothing else, and Tiffany didn't drink at all. She hated not being in control, so any sort of substance abuse was out of the question to her."

"So what vices did she have?"

"What do you mean?"

"We all have vices. If hers wasn't alcohol or drugs, what was it?"

"Men," Julianna replied softly. "She wasn't into serious relationships, but she liked to tease men—she liked to get attention from them."

"Did she ever get on anyone's bad side that way?"

"Oh yeah. I used to worry about it. She could be really cruel to those guys, real cold. She'd flirt with them and tease them and then just get bored and walk away like nothing happened. That seriously annoyed a lot of men, especially the kind she liked."

"What was her type?"

"Professionals with money to burn. The kind of guys who get their egos wounded real quick."

Wildow nodded. "Do you think someone she dated and then dumped might have wanted to do this?"

"Yes," Julianna replied, nodding her head as she burst into tears. "I was always telling her to be careful and not get herself into trouble with these guys. When we first started talking, I thought she was just into playing hard to get. We used to discuss guys, since she was single and I'm divorced, and it was like a pastime to compare what we did and didn't like in a man. Tiffany knew what she liked, but it was just to tease. I warned her to cut it out before something bad happened, but I never thought anything like this could be possible."

Wildow handed Julianna a tissue as she dissolved into sobs. "I know this is hard for you, but do you know the names of any recent boyfriends, or any who were particularly disgruntled?"

Again Julianna nodded, trying desperately to stifle her sobs. "Yeah. His name is Alex and he's a manager of some big corporation. I don't know much else about him, but I know he was starting to scare Tiffany. When she tried to break it off with him, he wouldn't take no for an answer. He started to follow her around, stalking her. He sent her flowers and candy, begging her to come back. She put the flowers in a vase and ate the candy, but still ignored Alex. Then he started sending her voice mails, dozens in a day sometimes. She finally called him back and told him to leave her alone, but I guess he didn't listen, because she said she was seeing his car following her everywhere. One morning she said it was parked outside her house, and he was inside it smiling as he looked up at her bedroom window."

"How long ago was this?"

"About a week and a half ago. She told him she was going to get a restraining order if he didn't stop, but I don't think she ever did. She was too busy to get involved with legal stuff."

"Do you have a description of the car?"

Julianna shook her head. "No."

"When was the last time you saw her?"

"Last week, on the Tuesday before Thanksgiving. Tiffany and I had schedule changes so we didn't see each other as much, but she looked good on Tuesday. She said Alex had been backing off. She was upset about the security cameras though. We're always having trouble with them here. They never work. She said that she was going to give Konrad a piece of her mind, which basically meant that she was going to yell at him."

"Who's Konrad?"

"He's the head security guard for the studio."

"Did she frequently have trouble with him?"

"Other than being mad about the broken cameras, no. Konrad's a good guy. I've never seen him do anything to Tiffany or anyone else that would raise an eyebrow."

"Is there anything else you think would be relevant to this case?"

Julianna shook her head. "No, not that I can think of right now."

"Well, thank you for your time. We'll be in touch if we need to speak to you again."

"Man, I wasn't even here last night!" Konrad Stewart declared when questioned about Tiffany. His dark face was aglow with stress. His muscular build looked out of place seated on a small chair in the dingy security office.

"I didn't say you were," Zenoni replied, "but I do want to know where you were, since I've got a source telling me that you and Tiffany had an altercation last week."

"I didn't have an altercation with anybody, okay? Tiffany had a bad temper. She found out some of the cameras weren't working, got mad, and took it out on me, since I'm the head guard."

"How did she notice the cameras weren't working, and why weren't they working?"

"She said she didn't see the little red lights blinking, so she must have been looking to check. She did that sometimes. I can't tell you why they don't work all the time—they're old. This isn't exactly a first-rate studio."

"Who was in charge of fixing them?"

"The janitors."

"I've never heard of janitors fixing security cameras."

"It's to save money. When the cameras break, the janitors are ordered to fiddle around with them."

"Are they successful?"

"They must be; the cameras *do* work sometimes. If I see that they aren't working correctly during my shift, I'll check it out. Most of the time they are just shut off. I don't know why—maybe because of age. After a certain amount of time, they just burn out until someone manually adjusts them again. I told Mr. Genson—the manager—to get new ones, but I guess he didn't think it fit into the budget."

"You said you're the head of security. How many other guards are there?"

"Only one full time, the night-shift guy, Nelson Rosley. He might be here now. He was just going off duty when I arrived, and by then the body had been found. We also have two part-time guys who work on the days Nelson and I have off. They're not here now, but their names are Elijah Berenski and Winston Hamilton."

Zenoni nodded, as he noted the guards' names. "What time did you leave here last night?"

"I'm here from eight in the morning until seven at night."

"So I presume Nelson is in from seven to close?"

"Yeah, close is usually around three in the morning, since the last show goes off the air at two, but it takes a while to shut down for the night. Nelson is supposed to work until three."

"So last night, after you left the studio, what did you do?"

"I went to get dinner at Edith's Place—a hamburger joint near my house—and then I went home. I was in my house from about nine until six this morning when I left for work."

"Can anyone confirm you were home?"

"No. I live alone. I'm not lying to you, Detective."

"I never said you were. So when was the last time you saw Tiffany alive?"

"As I was leaving last night, she was storming around the back room. She was upset about the inventory files; they must have been messed up or something."

Again Zenoni nodded. "Was she angry at anyone?"

"I think the situation in general had her annoyed. She was talking to herself mostly, but I bet she was looking to yell at Arnold—Mr. Genson—as soon as she saw him."

"All right. Thank you for your time, Mr. Stewart. You've been very helpful. Is there anything else you'd like to add?"

"Just that I hope you get whoever did this."

"We will."

Nelson Rosley was a grossly overweight middle-aged man with a pasty complexion, thick glasses, long dirty-blond hair, and shifty eyes. He looked out of place in the janitors' break-room, the first suitable area the police had found to conduct the interview. He was obviously nervous about being flanked by police and, although he was trying desperately to disguise his fear, his finger twiddling and toe tapping gave him away.

"Wowza! So . . . she's dead, huh?" he declared in response to the news of Tiffany's demise.

Nolan Wildow had been a homicide detective for close to twenty years and he had worked many cases during the time, yet never before had he heard a reaction quite like Nelson's. The oddly conversational—almost pleasant—tone of voice and informal choice of words shocked the detective into temporary silence. When he did mange to find his voice, he simply replied, "Yes, Mr. Rosley, I'm afraid she is."

"Bummer. Tiffany was okay. She got mad at me once for calling her Tiff, but other than that, she was okay. Just a little feisty."

"Did you know much about her?"

"Not really. Just that she was good at her job."

"Did you see her often?"

"From time to time around the studio."

"Were you working last night?"

"Yeah, why?" Nelson asked quickly. His eyes were suddenly startled; they peered out from behind thick glasses, giving the impression of a helpless owl.

"I need to know if you saw or heard anything."

"No, nothing."

"Why were the security cameras broken?"

"What?"

"There's no footage from last night; the cameras were broken. You must have known that."

"Well, I only work to a certain time; the studio doesn't require a guard in the wee hours of the morning. This place has alarm systems; a guard only has to be on duty while others are in the active studio."

"Strange way to run things."

Nelson nodded, but said nothing.

"I'm still confused though, Mr. Rosley. How could you

have failed to notice the cameras weren't working while you were on your shift?"

"Well, I . . . um . . ."

"This is a murder investigation. If you fail to be truthful there will be consequences."

"I fell asleep, okay? I work six days a week and I've got three kids at home, all under the age of five, and my wife is diabetic. My life is high stress. The body needs to sleep! Nothing ever happens here at night, okay? Even those protesters are gone! So I doze off every once in a while—what's the harm? I need this job, really. I don't even got a high school diploma so, considering that, this place is a lucky break."

Wildow sighed. "Okay, so you saw and heard nothing?"

"No, I swear I don't know anything about this! I will admit though, I left later last night, around four in the morning, because I had been out cold from about one and woke up late. But I didn't see or hear anything."

"Okay then, Mr. Rosley."

"Can . . . can I go?"

"Yes, you can. We'll be in touch if we have any more questions."

There were six cameramen employed by the studio. Five of them were no help to the investigation. The sixth was Ryan Donnik, a scruffy, college-aged brunet with a nasty attitude. He was identified as the man who had been eager to speak to the press earlier in the morning. Looking at him, Zenoni was reminded of his nephew, Denise's son Vincent, who walked through life wearing a similar devil-may-care sneer.

"Hello, Ryan, I'm Detective Zenoni. I'm here to ask you some questions about the murder that took place here late last night or early this morning."

"Okay," Ryan replied calmly, as he slouched in his chair. His pants sagged on his bony frame; they were at least three sizes too large.

"I hear you were pretty eager to talk to reporters this morning. Does that mean you have substantial information about the victim, Tiffany Kehl?"

"Well, kinda," Ryan replied, not even attempting to suppress a yawn. "Mostly I just wanted to get on TV; this is big news, man. You gotta admit it's wicked cool."

"You find the idea of murdered young women cool?"

"Well I don't mean it like *that*," Ryan exclaimed, somewhat defensively. "I just mean that something actually *happened*. Not much does around here."

"What did you know about Tiffany?"

"Not a lot, dude. I know she was annoyed with her boyfriend."

"Why do you say that?"

"I walked outside one night and she was fighting with this guy in a car."

"Description?"

"He was white, dark hair, and looked like he was in his thirties. The car was a Cadillac, a new one. It was dark outside, so I couldn't really see the color, but I'm almost positive it was either black or blue."

"Did you get a plate number?"

"Nope."

"Anything else?"

Ryan shook his head.

"You've been helpful to us and I thank you for that, but I'd advise against saying anything to the press."

"Sure," Ryan replied, not managing to lose his sneer. "Can I leave now?"

Zenoni nodded and Ryan strutted toward the door, slamming

it shut behind him. The detective had the sinking feeling that his warning would not be followed.

Zenoni and Wildow met in the hall and compared notes for what seemed like the millionth time that day.

"At least you got some kind of identification on the boyfriend's car and his looks," Wildow declared, staring down at his own notes.

"I'm going to request that the two part-time guards be located," Zenoni replied. Let's see if we can question them down at the station. Who knows, they might have some information. I'd also like to see what we can find out about her college situation as soon as possible. I want to speak to that professor and classmate."

Wildow nodded in agreement and added, "Let's go talk to her parents now. I got a lead on where they live. Provided they haven't been watching the local news, we'll be able to gauge their response. Then we can head over to Tiffany's place and see if we can find any clues in her house."

Zenoni nodded and started toward the studio exit. Breaking the news of a death to loved ones was the worst part of his job, especially when the deceased was a twenty-six-year-old who had everything to live for.

This one's gonna be tough, he thought, as he exited the studio. *One of the toughest.*

Chapter Three

The detectives took Zenoni's black Chevy Impala to the location of Tiffany's home, leaving Wildow's car at the studio for the time being. Zenoni drove with a tight knot in his stomach; it was impossible for him to break the news of a loved one's death without putting himself in the family's shoes.

If someone told me Lorraine had been murdered, I'd have a nervous breakdown, he thought to himself, trying desperately to push his emotions aside as he gripped the steering wheel tighter and pushed his foot down on the accelerator.

His GPS informed him that he was at the Kehl house: a large, decorative, stucco structure, the color of beach sand. It was big without being gaudy, the kind of place that people who were living comfortably—yet just missed the title of wealthy—inhabited. The spacious front lawn was dotted with evergreen shrubs, manicured so perfectly that it could only be the work of lawn-care professionals. Vaguely, Zenoni wondered what the garden looked like in full bloom.

The assets of the house were lavish: grand windows with white sills, marble steps leading up to the porch, and a red-tiled roof. A new Mercedes Benz sedan was parked in the cobblestoned driveway. The license plate read DRFEET.

"Amy was right about Tiffany's old man being a podiatrist," Wildow remarked, staring at the plate on the cream-colored luxury car that Zenoni had parked behind.

Within seconds the detectives were standing at the front porch, ringing the doorbell. The buzzer echoed through the house for about ten seconds before a tall woman in her early sixties opened the door. From the first glance, it was obvious that she could be no one other than Tiffany's mother; the resemblance was striking. They were approximately the same height and had the same eyes, nose, and jaw line. In a final touch of irony, the woman at the door also wore a pink sweater, although it was a lighter shade than her daughter's.

Evelyn Kehl did not look happy about coming to the door without makeup and dressed in what women of her stature might consider "shabby house-things," but her look of mild annoyance turned into tension when she saw the badges that Zenoni and Wildow were holding up.

"Evelyn Kehl?" Zenoni questioned.

"Y-yes?" the woman stammered, her blue eyes wide with worry.

"I'm Detective Zenoni and this is my partner, Detective Wildow. Do you mind if we come in for a minute?"

Evelyn asked no questions; she simply nodded and led the detectives into a modern high-tech living room that was dominated by a massive flat-screen television. The glare from the game show currently on the screen reflected off the shiny hardwood floors. The white walls were dotted with Monet prints and photos of Tiffany. Looking at them deepened the already considerable ache in Zenoni's stomach.

As the detectives observed the Kehl's living room, a man descended the staircase. He was in his late sixties or early seventies, but his light eyes were as sharp as his white-haired crew cut. Thomas Kehl was in good shape for a man his age, but Zenoni assumed that his impending announcement would change that.

"Who are you?" the man asked as he stared at the two police

officers. This time Wildow voiced the introductions, followed by a request to have the Kehls sit down. Once seated on their plush, cream-colored leather couch, Evelyn's worry sprang forth.

"What's happened?" she almost screamed as she gripped her husband's hand so hard that her knuckles turned white. Her enormous eyes looked from one detective to another, pleading for reassurance.

"I'm sorry I have to say this to you," Zenoni began, as gently as he could. "This morning your daughter, Tiffany, was found dead in her workplace."

The color instantly drained from Evelyn Kehl's face, making her look like a ghost. Beside her, her husband's eyes were wide, shocked, and disbelieving.

"It can't be!" she cried, vigorously shaking her head from side to side. "Not Tiffany—no, no, no, no, *no!*" Her last word broke off into a howl of anguish and she collapsed into her husband's arms, sobbing hysterically.

Thomas Kehl appeared to be shell-shocked. For several minutes, he simply held his wailing wife and stared at the detectives, dumbfounded. In her grief and denial, Mrs. Kehl was unwittingly giving the lawmen an ample amount of background information on her daughter.

As she sobbed, she declared that Tiffany *couldn't* be dead. Tiffany was too good, too *promising* to be dead. It *must* be someone else's child, not Tiffany. She had been obsessed with jewelry since discovering her grandmother's collection at age four. She was an assiduous teenager who had sacrificed time with friends so she could work counters at local jewelry stores and learn all she could about precious and semiprecious stones. She had been a good girl, a perfect little angel, and she could *not* be dead. After that declaration, grief overtook Evelyn Kehl.

"She needs to be sedated," Thomas remarked, gripping his

wife tightly. Zenoni nodded and used his radio to call an ambulance for the grieving mother.

"I'm very sorry this happened," Wildow said earnestly, as they awaited the ambulance. "I assume that Tiffany was an only child."

"Well, she was *our* only child," Thomas replied, his voice and eyes oddly distant. "Evelyn was married once before—disastrously I might add—and she has a daughter from that marriage."

"Were Tiffany and her sister close?" Zenoni questioned, grappling for his notepad.

Thomas shook his head. "Half-sister, and no. Tiffany was always responsible, mature, and driven. She was an angel. Christina was anything but. She's moody, always talks back, and has no direction in life. She would fight with anyone about anything and she resented Tiffany like nothing else."

"Oh?" Wildow replied, his interest piqued. "Where is Christina now?"

"I have no idea," Thomas replied. "She was a handful and she left home at eighteen. We haven't heard from her since and I think that's for the best."

"How old is Christina?"

"Four years older than Tiffany, so she's thirty. And, if you're going to look for her, I'd suggest looking under the name Christina Norrah—that was her father's last name. I gave her the Kehl name when I legally adopted her, but she never took to it."

"And you have no idea where she is now?"

"None. She could be in China for all I know. I doubt she'd be into traveling abroad though. She's hung around with a shady group ever since she was young. We tried to help her, but she'd have none of it. She was unbelievably headstrong."

Zenoni nodded as he took notes. Every so often he would

glance at Mr. Kehl, whose face was losing color. The awful news was starting to sink in, even if he was babbling about the wrong daughter. "Do you know if Tiffany kept in touch with Christina at all?"

Much to Zenoni's surprise, Evelyn Kehl reared up and answered the question for her husband. *"Never!"* she screeched hysterically, all her sophistication gone. "My Tiffany would *never* speak to Christina! She knew about all the trouble that little witch caused us and all the pain she put us through! Tiffany was a good daughter and she wouldn't bring that destructive *thing* back into our lives! Just go into her room and you'll see the kind of girl she was, my precious little baby . . ."

Once again, she dissolved into sobs as the detectives exchanged a conspiratorial glance. Neither of them had ever heard a parent speak about a child in such a way before. Thankfully, ambulance sirens were audible in the distance, so the anguished woman would soon be tended to.

"Your daughter had a room here?" Zenoni asked.

"Yes," Thomas replied, craning his neck to look out the window at the arriving ambulance. "Her childhood room. We never changed it. We turned Christina's old room into an office, but Tiffany's we left alone, since she sometimes stays over here around the holidays."

"Do you mind if we take a look around?"

"No, I'll show you the way as soon as Eve is taken care of."

Five minutes later, the paramedics sedated the hyperventilating mother and prepared her for a trip to the hospital, as Thomas led the detectives upstairs and down a long corridor brightened by skylights. The walls on both sides were filled with framed photographs of Tiffany at various ages. The retired podiatrist's pace was quick. He was anxious to get back downstairs to ride to the hospital with his wife.

The white wooden door at the very end of the hallway was

Tiffany's. Her name was spelled out across the wood in large block letters of alternating pink and purple.

"We got those letters when she was two," Thomas explained, as he grasped the door handle—gold plated with a glass doorknob shaped like a diamond.

"She loved this doorknob ever since she was small," he added, as he opened the door. "It's funny that she grew up to like gems so much," he continued. "She was named Tiffany because that's the store I bought her mother's engagement ring in."

Tiffany's room was a sea of pastel colors, glass figurines, and stuffed animals. The space seemed completely unchanged from her childhood years. On the far side of the room stood a bookcase filled with children's stories and college textbooks. Eyeballing the shelf quickly, Wildow noticed that most of the children's books had to do with buried treasure and the textbooks concerned the marketing of gemstones. The walls were covered in various wildlife posters.

"She liked animals, didn't she?" Wildow remarked.

"Sure did," Thomas replied, as he leaned against the doorway, slightly shaking, still in shock. "I want to ask you to please bring Amber to us. We'll take care of her and I know that's what Tiffany would have wanted." Once again, his voice quivered.

"Amber? Is that the dog's name?" Wildow questioned.

Thomas nodded.

"When was the last time you saw Tiffany?"

"On Thanksgiving. She spent the entire day with us."

"And where were you last night between two and three in the morning?"

"Here, sleeping. Why?" Thomas asked sounding defensive to the point of being angry.

"No reason."

"Don't patronize me. Why ask a question you don't need an answer to?"

"Was Tiffany always this tidy or have you cleaned in here since her last visit?" Zenoni interrupted, distracting Thomas.

"We dust it every so often, but Tiffany was a neat freak, so this place was always orderly. She was such a good girl—never any trouble. I can't believe this happened to her. Christina, sure, but not Tiffany. She had no enemies. Everyone loved my little angel."

And suddenly, as if just realizing what had happened, Thomas Kehl burst into tears.

Chapter Four

After leaving the Kehls' residence, Zenoni and Wildow drove to Tiffany's address and discussed the case on the way.

"I've heard of parents favoring children, but that's unbelievable," Zenoni declared, referring to the way the Kehls had spoken of Christina.

"No wonder the other girl left home so early," Wildow replied. "And what about the father? It took him long enough to break down."

"Well, the death of a loved one can be a great shock," Zenoni replied, remembering when his father died and how it had taken him a full three days to grasp that the man he had been so close to was gone forever.

"That's true. I keep thinking her job has something to do with it, though. There are too many strange characters there."

"You're telling me," Zenoni replied. "And this mystery boyfriend of hers sounds more than a little creepy."

Wildow nodded. "When we get back to the station, it will be interesting to see what we find on these people's background information."

Zenoni nodded as Wildow switched on the radio. Lynyrd Skynyrd's "Free Bird" blasted over the speakers and Wildow happily bobbed his head to the beat. When they had first started working together Zenoni had found his partner's fondness for

44

classic rock annoying. Now he was used to it and drove, without comment, toward the next destination of their investigation.

The ever-trusty GPS informed the detectives that they were at Tiffany's apartment as Zenoni made a right turn off the main avenue into the parking lot of a modern condominium complex. The white concrete structures were two stories high with open terrace hallways leading to doors marked with gold numbers. Outside was a large parking lot with numbered spots full of parked cars. A large green wooden sign with white posts stood near the entrance declaring WELCOME TO MAPLE COVE CONDOMINIUMS in bold gold letters.

The complex was well cared for and covered in foliage. Trees sprang up from every corner with bird feeders hanging from various branches. It was a nice place, but not particularly extravagant—not half as ritzy a residence as Zenoni was sure Tiffany had dreamed of living in.

The detectives drove to a row of spots labeled GUEST PARKING and shut off the car abruptly, ending the final guitar riffs of "Free Bird." Directly in front of the guest parking area was the office for the property.

Although the gray morning clouds had cleared into sunshine, there was no warmth in the air. Zenoni's ears were numb with cold as he rang the office doorbell. He regretted forgetting his hat in the morning rush and envied Wildow, who was standing beside him, bundled up, and experiencing no such issues. Luckily, almost as soon as he rang the bell, a woman's voice chimed "Who is it?" from behind the door.

"Police!" Zenoni bellowed, as he held his badge up to the peephole, prompting a swift unlocking and opening of the door. A short, plump woman with frizzy bottle-blond hair appeared before them. She wore an electric blue sweater with a smiling pink cartoon cat on it. Although she was well into her sixties, she made an effort to look younger with heavy makeup and bright red manicured nails. Her eyes were wide with surprise and worry.

"Hello, ma'am, I'm Detective Zenoni and this is my partner, Detective Wildow. Do you mind if we come in for a minute?"

Wordlessly, the woman removed herself from the doorway and allowed the detectives into the blissful warmth.

"Are you the owner of this complex?" Zenoni asked, grateful that his teeth had stopped chattering.

"Well, yes, I mean, I'm one of them. It belongs to my husband and me," she replied, her nasal voice sounding on edge.

As if on cue, a short, stocky, balding man entered the room. Around the same age as the woman, he dressed in a casual black tracksuit, and was limping badly.

"Who is it, Joyce?" he bellowed, not waiting for a reply. "Whoever you are, be patient. My back gave out last night since the missus took me dancing. I told her we were too old but—" His cheerful voice and wide smile vanished when he saw the badges the two men held before him.

"Who are you?" he asked, his face taut with tension.

Once again, Zenoni made the introductions before diving into the big question.

"Was a woman by the name of Tiffany Kehl a resident here?"

"Not was, she *is*," the woman replied, a note of curiosity under the initial suspicion. "Why?"

"Miss Kehl was found dead this morning at her place of employment."

"How horrible!" the woman cried, clearly upset, but Zenoni thought, also somewhat relieved that the police weren't there due to any personal misfortune of hers.

"How?" the man asked, his face a mask of shock.

"The official autopsy report has yet to come back, but it looks like she was beaten to death," Wildow replied.

"Murdered?" the woman exclaimed, shocked.

Wildow nodded. "It certainly looks that way."

"Can I have your names, please?" Zenoni asked, taking advantage of the sudden silence, grasping for his pad and pen.

"I'm Joyce and he's Morry. We're the Knavs," the woman replied, her voice shaking slightly.

"When was the last time you saw Tiffany?"

"I suppose it was about three days ago," Morry replied. "You know how it is in these complexes; people come and go and you might not see your neighbors for weeks."

"Do you live here too?"

"No. We're just the landlords. We live on Lilly Pad Lane, two towns over. We're here every day though."

Zenoni nodded. "Do you know of anyone who might have wanted to hurt Tiffany?"

"No!" Joyce cried immediately. "If we did, we would have warned her or . . . or . . . something!"

"Did she have trouble with anyone in this complex, even if it was something minor?"

"Well, there were a few small complaints," Morry replied, sounding somewhat uncomfortable. "Mrs. Pickerson—Ilene's her first name—she came home from shopping one day in a terrible mood because Tiffany had parked her car crooked and she—Ilene, I mean—couldn't get into her spot, which was right beside Tiffany's. Ilene's an early bird; she said she left around seven in the morning to shop and came back around ten. Tiffany must have worked all night and got home that morning half asleep."

"How long ago was this?"

"About two months back. Ilene came to me yelling and screaming, demanding that I do something about Tiffany's car."

"Do you know if Ilene confronted Tiffany herself?"

"I know she didn't. She's afraid of Amber—that's Tiffany's little dog. Truthfully, Ilene just likes having someone to yap at. Her husband's dead now, you know. It's probably the first time he's had any peace since the wedding."

Suppressing a snicker, Zenoni asked what had been done about the car.

"Well, I had no other choice. I had to go upstairs and ask her to move it. She complied, but she wasn't happy about it. She and Ilene had a little shouting match right there on the street, but it wasn't anything serious. Tiffany had a fast temper and she lashed out if her feathers were ruffled."

"Did she have issues with Ilene after that?"

"Not that I know of."

"How about other neighbors? Do you recall any other arguments?"

"Blanche complained about her a few times, but Blanche complains about everyone."

"Okay, tell us about Blanche, starting with her last name."

"Her name is Blanche Jiranek. She lives downstairs from Tiffany. Truthfully, I think that's—or that *was*—part of the problem. Tiffany has—had—the nicest apartment in this place. Blanche has the cheapest and is barely holding on to that. So I think there was some jealously there."

"She's a single mother, you know," Joyce added, as if this was the most crucial piece of information.

"Anyway," Morry continued, shooting his wife a don't-interrupt-me look, "Blanche was in here a few times complaining that Tiffany made too much noise upstairs and her son couldn't sleep. The kid's name is Lawrence; he's a sickly little guy."

"How did Blanche say Tiffany made too much noise?"

Morry shrugged. "She told me she walked around the house in her high heels, stomping heavily just to annoy her. She also said she talked so loud on the phone that she could hear the conversations. Mostly she complained about the dog barking too much."

"What did you do about the complaints?"

"Nothing. This is pet-friendly housing and Blanche knew that when she moved in."

"That's one thing that can be said for Tiffany," Joyce declared suddenly. "I didn't know her too well, but she liked animals as much as we do. I saw her putting food into the bird feeders outside more than once. She might have been a little arrogant, but she always paid her rent on time. She was no trouble to us."

"We're going to need to see her apartment," Wildow announced. "Do you have a way to unlock the door? She had her keys on the scene and they're being kept as evidence."

Joyce nodded. "Yes, we have spare keys to all the apartments. I'll get you Tiffany's."

"Why do you need to get in there?" Morry asked, genuinely curious.

"To see if anything there can be helpful to the investigation, and we need to get the dog. Tiffany's parents want to adopt it."

Morry nodded, satisfied with the answer.

"And we'll need to talk to the neighbors."

"That's fine. Most of them are home if you knock on the doors. Ilene is on the right side of Tiffany, number 43. Blanche is directly downstairs but she's probably not home at this time."

"You said you were out dancing last night, right?" Zenoni questioned curtly, as he stared suspiciously at the leg Morry favored.

"Yes. Why?"

"Where were you dancing?"

"At the Roasting Rodeo. That's the new southern cooking place over in West Brook."

"What time was this?"

"We were there from around eight until eleven. Just what are you implying?" Morry demanded, his voice at a near shout.

"Just running through the regular questions," Zenoni answered, forcing a smile. "Thank you for your help. It's greatly appreciated."

Ten minutes later the detectives walked along the second-floor terrace hallway toward what had been Tiffany's home. As soon as they were three feet from the door, Amber began to bark. It was a yapping sound that grated on the law enforcers' nerves.

"No wonder the neighbors complain," Wildow commented as Zenoni opened the door. Wildow was a dog lover by nature, but even he had to admit that Amber's noisiness was extremely annoying. The very second they walked across the threshold, a small orange-brown furball lunged toward them. It nipped at the cuffs of their pants and growled furiously before running and hiding under a coffee table. Despite repeated attempts to calm the animal, the dog showed no indication of becoming silent, so the detectives surveyed the house over the noise.

The living room looked like it had been professionally decorated. The walls were white, but covered with colorful abstract artwork. Most of the furniture was either glass or wood that was tinted so dark it looked black. The floors were hardwood, but covered in carpeting in the same style and colors as the art on the walls. It was a modest-sized apartment in a humble location, but it reflected a taste for the finer things in life.

"If she kept moving up in her job, she'd be out of here

soon," Wildow commented as he examined Tiffany's expensive stereo system.

Zenoni nodded. Like Tiffany's childhood room, everything was neat and tidy. The only items out of place were the many dog toys that littered the floor. Despite its impressive appearance, the living room had very few personal touches. On the glass coffee table beside the black leather couch stood a framed photo of Tiffany and her family at an amusement park. Zenoni guessed Tiffany was about eight years old. She and her parents smiled widely into the camera, while a sullen preteen girl with raven hair stood beside them, a pout on her pale face.

"I think we've got a description of the sister here," Zenoni said, pointing to the photograph.

That lone family photo was the only one containing human subjects. About twenty other photographs decorated the walls, tables, and shelves of the house—all of them depicting Amber: under the Christmas tree amid a sea of squeaky toys; in a pumpkin outfit under a HAPPY HALLOWEEN sign; and, as a puppy, sleeping under a large tree in a park.

As usual, Zenoni learned a lot about his victim by searching her house. Her closet was filled with expensive clothes, shoes, and handbags—all neatly arranged and sorted by color. Her bathroom boasted a wide array of quality cosmetics and her bathtub contained a Jacuzzi. But it was the kitchen he found most interesting, equipped as it was with top-of-the-line appliances and tabletops clean enough to sparkle in the sunlight.

It looks a lot better than my kitchen, Zenoni reflected, somewhat forlornly, as he thought of the colored pencils strewn across his kitchen table.

Despite the fancy cooking equipment, the contents of Tiffany's refrigerator informed Zenoni that she wasn't keen on preparing meals for herself. About five doggie bags from restaurants sat, never to be eaten, on the immaculately clean shelves. Diet shakes sat on the shelves in the dozens; apparently Tiffany had taken dieting seriously, despite the box of chocolate ice cream in the freezer. On the floor beside the fridge sat a light pink dog bowl in the shape of a crown, the magenta letters in its center declaring THE QUEEN EATS HERE. The dog bowl complemented the magnets on the fridge, most of which boasted the names of animal charities that Tiffany donated to.

"Adopt a Pet, Save the Whales, Guiding Eyes for the Blind—this girl had a penchant for giving money to animal-rights causes," Wildow exclaimed as he eyeballed the considerable collection.

"And that's not the only revealing thing about our victim here," Zenoni replied, pointing to a Pomeranian photo calendar he found pinned to the wall. "Look at the square on the fourth of November."

Wildow looked and saw that *Call Christie* was neatly scrawled within the space. "If Christie is short for Christina, then it seems like she and her sister were closer than people thought."

"I think it's time to interview some neighbors."

"What about the dog?"

"I'll call in some patrol officers to deal with her. She's a bit too feisty for me."

Ilene Pickerson lived three doors down from Tiffany's apartment. She was well into her seventies and seemed to be the sort of woman who sustained herself on TV dinners, soap operas, and gossip. Although she appeared generally shocked by the news of Tiffany's death, a spark of excitement underlined her expression of condolence. Ilene was a slightly overweight wire-haired woman with more wrinkles on her face than could be counted. She was generous about letting the detectives into her home, which she shared with four cats, two goldfish, and the ashes of Jonathan, her late husband.

"I've never had police officers in my house before!" Ilene exclaimed excitedly, as she poured tea for the detectives . "Although it is awful news. Tiffany was so young!"

"Did you know her well?" Wildow asked, sipping the tea happily, despite the fact that he was a coffee drinker at heart.

"Not really," Ilene replied, seating herself on a well-worn loveseat opposite the couch where the detectives sat. "She wasn't very neighborly. She wasn't home much and she never attended the neighborhood block parties."

"We've heard some reports about you and her having an argument over a parking space."

"That was a long time ago!" Ilene shrieked. "It was no big thing. I just came home one day and she was parked all crooked so I couldn't get into my assigned spot. I paid extra for that spot and I have a right to it! I don't like to be confrontational so I marched right over to Mr. Knavs—he's the landlord here—and told him to say something to her. He tried to talk me out of it. I expected as much: he just loved the way Tiffany dressed. Luckily I was able to persuade him to help me by threatening to withhold the month's rent. That did the trick! Tiffany ended up moving the car, although she was rather rude about it. That one had a nasty edge to her personality, I tell you."

"Did you have any more trouble with her?" Zenoni asked.

"No, although I was upset about the way she acted about the parking thing for quite a while. Then just a few days ago, I saw her putting food out for the stray cats. That made me soften my opinion of her since I love cats."

"Do you have any idea of who might have wanted to do this?" Zenoni asked, setting down his cup.

"Not a clue," Ilene replied.

"Okay, one final question: where were you last night?"

The old woman's eyes widened in alarm. "Just what are you suggesting?"

"It's a standard question, Mrs. Pickerson, but we do need an answer."

"If you must know, I was at Trinity Chapel last night playing bingo. I came home around ten and went straight to bed. I'm not as young as I used to be and I don't stay up late."

"Well then, thank you, Mrs. Pickerson. You've been very helpful," Wildow stated as he stood up and walked toward the door. Zenoni followed.

"The news is very surprising—and horrid!" Ilene retorted, not without an undertone of glee. Even though she was quick to see them out of her home and slam the door behind them, Zenoni had a feeling that being questioned about a murder was the most exciting thing to happen to Ilene Pickerson in a decade, and it would, undoubtedly, be the topic of discussion for many bingo games to come.

Blanche Jiranek wasn't home when the detectives knocked on her door, but the patrolmen arrived to collect Amber. Curious neighbors were standing out on the terrace pointing at the patrol car and discussing its presence. Zenoni and Wildow took the opportunity to talk to as many of them as possible. The majority didn't know Tiffany at all, and the rest only in passing. No one had substantial information.

Amber was finally subdued after forty-five minutes of being chased. The officers emerged from the apartment looking exhausted, with the snarling dog in a carrying case. Zenoni guessed that this was one of the toughest tasks the young policemen in this sleepy suburb ever had to deal with.

Seeing that the dog had been captured, the detectives were about to get into their squad car when an old van, painted a dull red and sporting a deep gash on its back bumper, pulled into the complex driveway. Instinct told Zenoni this was his chance to speak to Blanche, and he always listened to his gut.

The van parked and a haggard-looking woman emerged. She may only have been in her late thirties, but she looked well into her fifties. Her black hair was streaked with gray and her face was covered with premature wrinkles. She wore a light-blue-and-white-striped waitress uniform. Her name gleamed on the nametag. Listlessly, she walked to the side of the van and opened the sliding door to remove a small boy from the vehicle. Zenoni assumed this was her son, Lawrence, and he looked every bit as sickly as Morry Knavs had said. He was about seven, but very small for his age, and impossibly pale and fragile looking. His gray eyes peered out at the world from behind thick glasses; a hearing aid was visible.

Despite the general excitement of the neighbors and the presence of a police car, Blanche made no attempt to see what was going on. Instead, she focused on unloading her son and making her way to her ground-floor apartment. Quickly, Zenoni approached with his badge outstretched.

"Blanche Jiranek?"

The woman turned around immediately with an annoyed look on her face. Her son stared inquisitively at Zenoni behind his thick glasses.

"Who's asking?"

"I'm Detective Zenoni. I'm investigating the death of a neighbor of yours, Tiffany Kehl."

"She's dead?" Blanche asked, setting Lawrence back down in his seat.

"I'm afraid she is, and we're treating it as a homicide. Did you know her well?"

"We met on occasion around the neighborhood, nothing personal."

"I have some sources who claim they saw you and her exchange words."

A look of disgust distorted Blanche's face. "People around

here just love to gossip, don't they? But, yes, we argued from time to time. Tiffany wasn't exactly the most considerate person on earth. I'm sorry she's dead, but she could be very obnoxious."

"Do you have any idea who might have done such a thing?"

"None. I work seven days a week and spend the rest of my time with my son's doctors. He's not well, you know. On average, I have to pick him up from school three times a week due to medical issues, and then I have to make up the time lost at work. That's my whole life."

"Do you recall why you and Tiffany argued?"

"I told you, she was tough to deal with, and even harder to live under. She stomped around her house in heels, came home at all hours, and slammed doors. She also argued with people over the phone as loudly as she possibly could. I heard her arguing with some guy named Arnold—apparently her boss—more times than I can count and she used to scream at someone named Christie constantly."

"Do you remember what the yelling was about in regard to Christie?" Zenoni asked, extremely curious.

"Mostly she shouted at her about acting her age and being more responsible. Of course, the language she used during those conversations totally defeated that message—you wouldn't hear it from sailors!"

"Did you ever see Christie?"

"No, I never saw any visitors at Tiffany's."

"Did you ever hear any particularly memorable phone conversation? Something that jumped out at you as being odd?"

"No. I tried to block out as much as I could, which wasn't easy with that dog of hers barking. It never stops—the noise is relentless." Then, as an afterthought Blanche added, "What will happen to the dog now that Tiffany is gone?"

"Her parents are going to take care of it."

A look of pure relief stretched across Blanche's face. "That's good. At least it isn't going to the pound or, worse, being left alone up there for days. Now, if you'll excuse me, I've got to get Lawrence into bed. He's had an asthma attack; it's been a very stressful day."

"Just one last question: where were you last night?"

Blanche turned and fixed Zenoni with a nasty glare. "At home, after working a double shift. I already told you I waitress seven days a week and my son is sick. I have a lot on my plate. By the time I get home I'm exhausted. I don't know what you're implying, but I don't like it!"

"It's just a general line of questioning, ma'am. I have to ask, because you were seen arguing with the victim."

"Well now you've asked, so I can be excused!" Blanche snapped, before picking up her son and walking to her apartment. Zenoni watched her with a mixture of suspicion and pity before turning and walking back to his patrol car.

"What a group!" Zenoni declared as he started up the car and headed onto the main road. On the radio, George Thorogood was declaring that he drank alone.

"The two neighbors don't have solid alibis and the landlords need to be checked out. Maybe we can find them on the restaurant security cameras if they were really there."

Wildow nodded. "This is a complex one, all right. I just got a call from headquarters; the two part-time security guards are there. They came in to talk to us. Let's loop back to the studio and pick up my car, and then get back to the station and see what they've got to say."

Zenoni nodded and pushed the pedal down further. He felt better when he was driving fast. He hoped the two guards would have something interesting to say.

Chapter Five

The police station was a sizable two-story concrete structure with an American flag flying high on the flagpole out front. As soon as Zenoni and Wildow walked into the building, Sandra Lewis, one of the police secretaries, approached them holding a bundle of paperwork. Although she was only in her mid-twenties, Sandra was excellent at her job.

"I was wondering when you'd get here," she said as soon as she spotted the detectives. "Two guys came in saying they are security guards over at that television studio. We put the first guy, Elijah Berenski, in Interview Room One. The second guy, Winston Hamilton, is in Room Two. We also got a lot of background reports for you to look at."

"Thank you," Zenoni replied and nodded to Sandra, who smiled as she walked past him, her two-toned pink manicured nails gripping the paperwork in her hands, her ice blue high heels rapping across the floor. At the back of the room, an old office television was tuned to the local news station. Reporter Melody Zielinski was standing in front of the jewelry studio telling viewers about Tiffany's murder.

They didn't even give her body time to get cold, Zenoni thought, suddenly angry at the quick pace in which the news allowed the announcement of death to reach local ears.

"It seems like they get stories on the news quicker and quicker these days," Wildow complained.

"At least there's a chance that someone will see the report and call in with information," Zenoni replied, although that rarely happened.

Putting the annoyance of the news report behind him, Zenoni decided to interview Berenski as Wildow went to see Hamilton. When Zenoni entered Room One, Elijah rose from his seat and extended his hand while giving the detective a wan smile. The man's friendly greeting was a rare reaction in a police interview room and Zenoni was happy to return the man's welcome.

"Thank you for coming down here today, Mr. Berenski. It's greatly appreciated," Zenoni said earnestly, after introducing himself.

"Is no problem to come here," Elijah replied with a slight Polish accent in somewhat choppy English. Zenoni reckoned he was around sixty-five and couldn't imagine him actually running down a criminal if one appeared while he was on his shift as a guard. "I hear from news that Tiffany is dead; a terrible thing."

"Did you know her well?"

Elijah shook his head. "I saw her sometimes since she worked late often. But I did not know her much."

"Did you ever see her, or someone around her, behaving oddly?"

"I saw her fight with janitor a number of weeks ago."

"Which janitor?"

"I do not know his name, but he is white and skinny—he usually has not nice look on face."

Zenoni nodded. That description fit Hector Harte perfectly. "Do you know why they were arguing?"

"He was cleaning floor in stock room. She lost box of gems and did not like him there. She said he was in way. She asked me to help her find lost box, but it was no use. She then yell at me."

"But you were trying to help her. Why would she shout at you?"

Elijah shrugged. "We didn't find what she was looking for. She was angry and I was there."

"Did the fight with the janitor turn physical? Was he trying to hit her?"

Elijah shook his head. "No, just shouting. If he had touched her, I would have stopped him."

"Okay, but aside from the fight with the janitor and the missing box of gems, you had not seen her or anyone around her acting strange?"

"No."

"Is there anything else you would like to add?"

"Only that it is sad when the young are taken from us."

Across the hall, in Interview Room Two, Wildow was speaking to Winston Hamilton. The man looked as old as time, but his mind was as quick as a whip and he was extremely cooperative.

"I felt bad when I heard about the death," Winston stated sadly. "My momma always said there was far too much evil in this world, and I think she was right. That's why I came down here as fast as I could. I know something that might be very important to your investigation."

"What's that?" Wildow asked, eager to hear what he had to say.

"I saw her fighting with a man."

For the next fifteen minutes, Winston explained that he had been on duty one night when Tiffany got a call on her cell phone. An argument that could be heard down the hall ensued until Tiffany, still clutching her phone, stormed past the security office and out of the building. Winston, who had been a prison guard for over twenty years, tentatively followed her outside and observed the scene.

"If there was any sign of serious trouble, I would have called the police immediately, but I didn't feel right about just letting her go out there without knowing if it was dangerous," he explained. "In the parking lot she was screaming at this man and although she seemed really angry he was undaunted. Every time she took two steps away from him he took three toward her.

"She was screaming: 'Why is it so hard for you to understand, Alex? I don't want you near me! Either you leave me alone or I'll have you arrested!' She came back in the studio and he had the nerve to try and follow her in—with a big smile on his face to boot! I blocked him and told him to leave or I would call the police. He wasn't happy about that. He stormed outside and drove away quickly. I didn't get his license plate number, but I saw a piece of his work identification card. He had it stuck in the front pocket of his shirt, and it said he works for a company called Travest. I don't know what or where that is, but I'm sure that was the name."

"Can you describe him?"

"In his thirties, kind of tall, but not strikingly so—maybe six feet. He was lanky, a white guy, black hair and brown eyes, clean-shaven and dressed well. When I saw him, he must have just come from work. He was wearing an expensive suit and silk tie. To tell you the truth, I was really surprised by his behavior. It was the exact opposite of how I would expect someone who dressed like that to act."

"Nothing people do surprises me too much anymore," Wildow replied. "Did you see anything else?"

"No."

"Did you get his last name by any chance?"

"Nope. I wish I had but I didn't."

Satisfied that the man was being truthful, Wildow ended the interview and shook Winston Hamilton's hand. After rising from his chair and escorting the man out of the room, Wildow made his way back to the office with notes in hand. He had a feeling that Zenoni was going to be very interested in the part-time guard's statement about Alex from Travest—whatever "Travest" was.

Zenoni *was* interested in Winston Hamilton's story, so interested that he retrieved Tiffany's cell phone from the evidence room and checked to see if anyone by the name of Alex was listed as a contact. The search was fruitless.

"She must have never programmed him in or deleted him," Zenoni remarked, shrugging. His Google search of the word *Travest* was more successful. Travest was a large computer software company with a number of firms in the tri-state area.

"So Tiffany's man is into computers," Wildow declared. "We'll get his description sent out and see if it matches anyone from a local firm."

"Sounds good to me," Zenoni replied, eager to see what the police database had to say about the people they had met earlier in the day.

"The complaints about the studio being underfunded were right," he declared, staring at his computer screen. "They didn't spend anything on background checks. Two of their employees have previous records. Hector Harte, the janitor, was arrested for petty thievery back in 1991 when he was barely twenty-two. He was released on bail. Konrad Stewart, the head security guard, has a juvenile record. It's sealed, though, so I can't see what for."

"How about the others?"

"Everyone else from the studio is clean. I'm going to check out the protesters now."

"You know, I've read about those so-called blood diamonds," Wildow remarked, never one to miss an opportunity to share his grab-bag of knowledge. "They do have somewhat of a point: there have been situations in Africa where people are used as slaves to mine diamonds and other gems. However, only about three percent of gems today are supposedly from illegal trades. So it seems as if the Simics might be overdramatizing the idea that the entire studio is full of bloody gems."

"It wouldn't surprise me," Zenoni replied. "They seemed pretty intent on staying out there just for the sake of argument. Let's see what the database has to say about them."

With the clicking of a few keys Zenoni brought the Simics' background information up on-screen. His eyes grew wide with shock. The Simics were filthy rich. Otto's father had been the founder of a banking corporation, and Otto, an only child, had been the sole beneficiary of his father's fortune. Ironically, Otto's wealth stemmed from the exact sort of big business which he, his wife, and their followers protested against.

"Now I've heard everything," Wildow exclaimed, as he leaned back in his chair. "An heir to a fortune protesting big money corporations, the source of his own wealth!"

"They really do have the money to put all those people in a hotel indefinitely," Zenoni replied, amazed. "The staff confirmed their presence! I guess they say truth really is stranger than fiction for a reason."

The detectives spent the next half hour looking through various alibis. Security camera footage confirmed that Arnold Genson had been at the bowling alley and the Knavs had been at the Roasting Rodeo restaurant.

"Well, at least we know some people were being truthful

with us," Wildow remarked as he scanned the security camera footage, which had been delivered to the station house.

"We need to track down the sister and this Alex guy," Zenoni replied.

"What about the professor?"

"Tomorrow is Wednesday, class day. I want to pay him a visit on campus during his regular hours. Let's see if he knows exactly who this other student is who keyed Tiffany's car. If she's there for class, we can interview her right there, kill two birds with one stone."

"Sounds like a plan," Wildow agreed. "I think we've done all we can here for the night. I'm going to get ready to head home."

Wildow rose from his chair, stretched, yawned, and made his way toward his desk to retrieve his coat. Zenoni followed his partner's lead, but before leaving for the evening, he handed Sandra descriptions of Christina and Alex.

"I'll send these to patrol," she replied, quickly glancing down at the paperwork before her. "As soon as anything comes up, I'll let you know."

"Thanks," Zenoni replied, zipping up his jacket. "I'll sleep well tonight knowing my information is in good hands."

Sandra rolled her eyes. "Lucky you. I'm here until the end of the hour. Before you leave, can you please sprinkle some food in for the fish?"

"Will do."

On his way to the door Zenoni approached the large office fish tank that was cared for by the secretaries, primarily Sandra. As he uncapped the food jar and sprinkled the small multi-colored flakes into the water, he stared at the three inhabitants of the tank: Sam, the sea snail; Angela, the angelfish; and Larry, the lionfish; all seemed as content as possible as they aimlessly drifted around the tank. The fish were relaxing to watch and sometimes, particularly during stressful cases, Zenoni envied their easy existence.

In my next life I'll be a fish, he decided. *No job, no interviews, no decorating, no relatives coming over and—most important—no worries about capturing killers.*

Smiling as he thought about life as a sea creature, Zenoni exited the station and began his journey home for the night.

Chapter Six

Zenoni pulled into his driveway and killed the engine. All day long he had anticipated walking into his warm house and sitting in front of the television to watch the *Sports News Special Report*. That simple plan was dashed the second he opened the front door and saw the condition of the living room.

Lorraine had brought every box containing Christmas ornaments that she could find out of the attic and the basement. From every corner, snowmen and reindeer smiled at him. Although the artificial Christmas tree had not been assembled, its metal stand stood in place near the window, pleading to be put together. Lorraine sat among a stack of boxes containing porcelain houses. She'd started collecting the figurines nine years ago when the company had introduced the series, and every year since she bought the newest pieces. Now the full collection occupied the entire span of the back wall. Napoleon was beside her, crouched down and swishing his tail, ready to attack a stack of boxes he was meowing at. Christmas music blasted from the radio. Zenoni supposed he would have to get used to it—from the day after Thanksgiving until the end of Christmas, the station played nothing but holiday tunes.

"You're home early," Lorraine chimed, as soon as she saw her husband.

"I thought you were working on your book today," he replied, staring at the maze of cardboard boxes scattered across the floor.

"Well, I was, but then I thought this was more important. Christmas only comes once a year and we're late getting started. I've got everything we have in the house here. We'll never have it all up by December first, but let's at least strive for the eighth, okay?"

"Sure," Zenoni replied as he walked into the kitchen and poured himself a glass of orange juice.

"So are you going to get the big stuff for the lawn out from storage soon?"

"Yes! I've said it a million times!"

"I'm sorry, Angelo, but you know it's important to get this done," Lorraine whined. "It's for charity."

Zenoni rolled his eyes and said nothing even though he knew his wife was right. Every year the Zenonis decorated their house elaborately. The sheer brightness of the lights caused a steady stream of admirers to appear. Noting how much attention their home was getting, Zenoni and Lorraine had eventually put a donation box in front of their house. Every year the earnings got bigger and all the proceeds were given to numerous charities. Although it was for a good cause, the tradition of decorating, which Zenoni had inherited from his Italian family, was becoming a major production. Every year the ornaments got bigger and more elaborate, and the very idea of standing on a ladder stringing lights onto the roof filled him with dread. His back wasn't as young, or as agile, as it used to be.

If I win the lottery I'll pay professionals to set everything up, he thought, hoping that the numbers would eventually come up in his favor.

"How was your day?" Lorraine asked, sensing that her husband was in no mood to discuss decorations.

"Hard," he replied, starting to unpack a box of ornaments

simply to have something to do. "We got a twenty-six-year-old woman, who had everything going for her, beaten to death. Wildow and I had to break the news to her parents; those poor souls are hysterical with grief, and so close to Christmas too."

"Any ideas on who did it?"

"Not yet, but we have lots of leads. She had some strange people at her job, trouble at her college, neighbor issues, and a creepy boyfriend."

"Sounds pretty hectic."

"It is. I'm going to solve this one, though. I have to. I can't get the look on her mother's face out of my mind. I can't bring Tiffany back, but I can at least give her family some closure."

"I wonder about this society sometimes," Lorraine replied sadly. "It seems all too easy for people to get in trouble."

"That's because it *is* easy to get in trouble. It's staying out of it that's hard."

Lorraine sighed and looked over at her husband. "Denise called today. Vincent's giving her a hard time again."

"What else is new?" Zenoni retorted, more harshly than he intended. Lorraine's sister had experienced increasingly serious behavioral issues with her son since the death of her husband, Frank, in a car accident after a night of drinking, five years before. Although Vincent was his nephew, Zenoni had never been particularly fond of the boy. From early childhood he had been a complainer and, as he got older, he had turned manipulative. Since his father died, Vincent had become so completely unruly that Denise's nerves were frayed to nearly nothing.

"He's hanging around with a bad crowd," Lorraine continued, as she pushed batteries into a snow globe. "Denise told me he doesn't come home until four in the morning, and he won't tell her where he's going or been. She thinks he's been drag racing."

Zenoni nodded his head but voiced no opinion. Vincent was

over eighteen and had legally bought his sporty little car with the trust fund money his father had left for him.

"He still has no interest in going to college or finding some sort of career or *anything*," Lorraine lamented. "Denise is afraid he's going to end up dead or in jail."

"I wouldn't be surprised."

"He's your nephew, Angelo. Is that really what you want to see happen to him?"

"I'm not saying it's what I *want* to see, but it wouldn't surprise me. He got his lousy attitude from his father."

Lorraine had no answer. She had not liked her brother-in-law any more than Angelo had. Lorraine had tried to persuade her younger sister not to marry Frank, but Denise had been too smitten to listen. Although Frank liked to say he was an electrician, most of his days had been spent betting on horses at the racetrack. Frank had been the sort of small-time crook with an inflated ego that set Zenoni's teeth on edge.

"Denise is worried about Mom and Dad finding out about the trouble Vincent's getting into. He's their only grandchild and you know how they worry. This would keep them from sleeping at night! They only come up here once a year. Do you think you could convince Vincent to behave himself at least until they leave?"

"I don't know, Lorraine. I'll try, but I can't promise you anything. You know how he is. Like his father, he doesn't listen to anybody."

Wordlessly, Lorraine ripped tape off another box and released more Christmassy contents from their cardboard prison. Behind her, Napoleon jumped in the vacant boxes and rolled amid the scraps of tissue paper. As he surveyed the less-than-tidy condition of his house, Zenoni sighed. Christmas was always a hectic holiday. Between decorating and family, he was surprised that he had managed to avoid a nervous breakdown.

He prayed he would have the murder case solved before Lorraine's parents arrived from Florida to stay in the spare bedroom until the week after Christmas. It was a family tradition, which required an abundance of planning, especially since Lorraine's father had a bad heart and her mother had issues with high blood pressure. Although both her parents were healthy enough to be champion shuffleboard players in their retirement center, Lorraine was protective of them and tailored their annual New York trips to be low on stress.

"How's Denise handling herself through all this again?" Zenoni questioned, thinking of the taut face and nervous disposition that his sister-in-law had possessed the last few times he had seen her.

"You know Denise. She tries to keep a smile on her face no matter how rough things get. I'm starting to worry about her, though. Her nerves are so bad now that she's having trouble holding onto the seamstress job. I wasn't a big fan of Frank, but thank God he left her that insurance policy, or I don't know where she'd be now."

"Well, you're a good, protective big sister to her," Zenoni replied, flashing his wife a small smile, which she returned. Despite her face being drawn with worry, Zenoni could still see traces of the young woman he had met when she was working in a Brooklyn bakery over thirty years before. Even back then, she and her sister had been close, so it wasn't surprising that Denise still spent most of her time calling Lorraine to report Vincent's latest misadventures.

"I've always liked Denise, you know that," Zenoni declared as he opened the box containing the artificial tree and began to separate the branches. "Before your parents arrive I'll talk to Vincent. I warn you though, it won't be easy to resist smacking the little brat upside the head."

"He can be hard to get along with, but have a heart, Angelo.

He misses his dad." There she went again, defending him like she always did, enabling him to act the way he did. She and Denise could always find an excuse, some outside reason, for Vincent's despicable actions.

The doorbell rang. Its harsh buzzer filled the air with discordant noise that made Napoleon jump high into the air and run, bushy-tailed, into the bedroom to hide.

"Dinner's here," Lorraine replied, groaning as she lifted herself off the floor to answer the door.

"You ordered in?" Zenoni asked, not surprised. Lorraine rarely cooked.

"Yeah, I forgot to mention I ordered Chinese food for tonight. I figured you'd enjoy General Tso's Chicken."

Zenoni grinned as Lorraine answered the door. One of the perks of being married so long was that she always knew just what kind of food to order for him.

Later, as they sat down for dinner surrounded by containers of white rice, dumplings, plastic plates, and Napoleon, who was meowing for shrimp, Lorraine asked if he thought the first forty-eight hours—the most important time in a case— were going well.

"So far we have leads, which is what matters, but we still have to see what the medical examiner says. So tomorrow I'll be confronted with the body . . . again." Zenoni handed Napoleon a shrimp and grew quiet. He hated dead bodies so much that he had trouble viewing an open casket at a wake. Although he enjoyed solving cases, he detested the sight of death. "How's the book coming along?" he asked suddenly, desperate to lighten the mood.

And so, for a little while, over takeout dinner amid Christmas decorations, Zenoni listened to his wife's progress with her children's book, feeling like an average man who had nothing to do with homicide investigations.

Chapter Seven

At exactly 9:14 A.M. the following day, Angelo Zenoni and Nolan Wildow arrived at the coroner's office. The morgue was located in the basement of Saint Lucille's Hospital. It was a drab space with the temperature set at a chilly fifty-five degrees. Tiffany's pale body lay on a metal gurney in the center of the room. Without makeup, she looked barely older than a teenager.

"She was pretty," Zhang Mingu, the coroner, declared as he stared at the body. Zhang was forty-seven, but looked twenty-five, and talked about action movies every chance he got. Zenoni often wondered how a talkative and entertainment-loving man like Zhang ended up choosing a career with cadavers, but he had worked with him many times and knew that he was excellent at his job.

"That she was," Zenoni replied. "How exactly was she killed?" He wanted to get the morgue meeting over with as soon as possible; the setting gave him the creeps and his unease was multiplying with every second spent in the room.

"She was bludgeoned to death, and judging by the shape of the wounds, I would say the lamp you found lying beside her was the murder weapon."

"How many times was she hit?" Wildow questioned.

"I'd say maybe two or three times."

"What's the approximate time of death?"

"Two or three A.M."

"Do you have any idea what height or strength the person who did this would have to be?"

"The blows to the head were pretty straightforward, so I would say whoever did this was around the victim's height—five foot six or so. There was an element of surprise with this attack, since she was hit multiple times on the back of the head. There's no evidence that she put up a fight. I'd say this could have been done by a man or a woman, as long as they were reasonably strong and enraged."

"That makes sense. We thought this was a personal crime from the start. Is there anything else you can tell us about the body?"

"Nothing much. She has a small scar on her left ankle; it's completely healed, but it was a pretty deep gash. I'd say she's had it since elementary school." Zhang looked down and shook his head. "At least she was hit on the back, so her family can have an open-casket funeral. Trust me, if this beating had been head-on, we'd have nothing to go by. I can't imagine what she did to make someone this angry with her."

"Anything else?" Zenoni pressed, his stomach queasy just thinking about what a full-frontal bashed-in head would look like, and his discomfort was clear.

"Bodies really bother you, don't they?" Zhang asked, unable to hide a slightly amused smile as he pushed the gurney back toward the freezer.

"Ever since I was little," Zenoni replied, remembering the way he used to hide from his parents whenever they told him he had to go to a wake or funeral. "I honestly have no idea how you handle this job."

Zhang uttered a small laugh. "Truthfully, it's boring. I'm hoping to retire early and maybe get a job as a special effects guy for a movie company."

Zenoni raised his eyebrows in a mix of disbelief and interest. "Seriously?"

"Sure. I could help create wax dummies. You know, like the ones they used in *Indiana Jones* or a disaster movie like *Independence Day.* Heck, I could even try my hand at some zombie films. There's been a lot of *Night of the Living Dead*–type stuff out recently. I took art classes in college and my uncle works in an independent film studio, so who knows?"

"Well, it sounds like you got some good leads," Zenoni replied and laughed. The idea of a coroner-turned-special-effects-man was amusing and somehow very fitting for a guy like Zhang.

"As of now, I'll leave the movies to the professionals and prepare this body to be released to the family. I tell you, out of all the bodies I've seen, no other one has been this pretty or this viciously murdered."

"There's a real sad edge to this case, that's for sure," Wildow replied, speaking for the first time since he arrived.

For a moment, all three men stood silently staring at the freezer, wondering how many dreams died with Tiffany. Then, silently, the detectives exited the morgue.

"Any news on the boyfriend's whereabouts?" Zenoni asked Sandra, as soon as he walked into the station.

Sandra shook her head, making her large gold hoop earrings jingle and shine in the sunlight that was radiating through the window behind her. "Nothing yet—we're checking the database for someone who matches the description, but Travest is a huge company and Alex is a common name. As soon as I hear anything you'll be the first to know."

"Okay, thanks," Zenoni replied and turned to walk away when Sandra held a newspaper out to him.

"Have you seen this?" she asked. "Page five. There's a story about the case, but it doesn't give too much away; it doesn't even name the detectives involved."

Zenoni took the paper and scanned the story. Sandra was right; it didn't give much information aside from the location of the murder and the victim's name, but he was still irked by the sensation that the press was hounding him. "They don't waste any time getting the word out, do they?" he asked, as he handed the paper back to the secretary.

Sandra shrugged. "At least it's just the *Long Island Local* and not *The New York Times,* so you don't have to worry about this ending up on Nancy Grace."

"That's true," Zenoni replied and smiled before walking over to Wildow, who was pouring himself a cup of water from the fountain. "There's still no ID on the boyfriend, but the press got ahold of the story; nothing substantial was leaked, though."

"So it's paperwork for the rest of the day," Wildow lamented before gulping down the last of his water.

"Yup," Zenoni replied. "Until it's time to pay her professor a little visit and hopefully speak to that classmate she was having trouble with too."

"It's gonna be a long day," Wildow exclaimed wearily, as he stretched his arms.

"At least we're making progress," Zenoni answered. "Besides, I can't say I mind too much, considering what's going on in my house. Working late means I don't have to spend the night untangling strings of lights and putting new batteries in the dancing Santa."

Chapter Eight

Zenoni and Wildow pulled into the vast parking lot of Holson University campus at 6:57 P.M. The class started at 8:00, and both detectives thought an hour was more than enough time to interview the professor. It was dark outside, so the parking lot was illuminated entirely by yellowish orange lights. Although it wasn't completely full, the lot housed a considerable number of vehicles. Holson University was known for its top-rated MBA classes. As he walked toward the campus' main building, Zenoni was reminded of his long-ago college years, which he spent surviving on a diet of pizza and sleeping two hours a night as he worked to earn his degree in criminal justice.

The detectives entered a large brick box of a building known as Kumble Hall and approached the security desk with their badges outstretched. After confirming who they were and their reason for the visit, Security pointed the law enforcers toward the information desk. The short-haired girl behind the counter was about twenty and seemed utterly amazed by the presence of the lawmen. Wildow asked her where Professor Mathis' class was held.

"Professor Mathis' marketing class is in the Business section—it's called the Kramer Building," she replied and handed the detectives a map of the campus. "His classroom is on the second floor, room 210. Do you want me to call ahead and tell him you're coming?" Her tone was polite, but her gray eyes were wide with curiosity.

"No, don't do that," Wildow replied quickly. "A little surprise might be more effective."

Flashing the young woman a hard smile, Wildow turned and exited the building, as Zenoni followed, gripping the map. Stepping outside was a shock to the system; the temperature seemed to be dropping by the second.

This is ridiculous. It's not even December and it feels like snow, Zenoni thought, as he stuffed his hands deep into his pockets for the duration of the walk.

"College brings back memories, doesn't it?" Wildow asked suddenly.

"Yeah, I guess," Zenoni replied. "For me it was mostly tests and classes. I lived at home, so I never got into too much."

"I lived at home too, but I had some moments in my youth, that's for sure. I remember one night me and some friends had a few beers and then ran through the sprinklers singing our rendition of 'Renegade.' It was near graduation, so most of the campus was partying. Ma had a fit when I got home soaked; she thought I'd been at a study group. She went on about the horrors of pneumonia for a good three days after that. She probably would have had a stroke if she knew I'd had beer too."

"Was it worth it?"

"Of course," Wildow replied, smirking. Zenoni chuckled. He always had trouble picturing Wildow, normally a serious man, letting loose in his youth—especially since he seemed so compliant to his domineering mother.

"You won't be running through any sprinklers tonight," Zenoni mused, watching the way his breath made clouds in the air.

"Never again. If Betty thought I'd ruined my good suit, I'd never hear the end of it."

Zenoni had to resist an amused smile. Betty, Wildow's wife, was a worrywart of the worst kind. If Lorraine was like her, Zenoni knew he would have gone crazy years ago. Wildow seemed to have a tolerance for overbearing women that eluded his partner.

It was a relief to get inside the Kramer Building and out of the frosty chill, yet the stairs to the second floor were steep. By the time the detectives reached the top landing, they were huffing and puffing, and even the walk down the corridor seemed like too great an effort.

So this is what old age is going to feel like, Zenoni thought, half amused, half sad, as he took note of the aches and pains in his legs.

The door to room 210 was ajar, exposing a portly man in a crisp brown suit sitting behind a large wooden desk. He was so intent on the paperwork he was studying that he did not appear to hear the detectives' approaching footsteps. Wildow reached out, rapped twice on the door, and strolled into the room as the man looked up.

"Edward Mathis?" Zenoni asked, extending his badge.

"Yes?" the startled man answered, fumbling to get his glasses out of his shirt pocket.

"I'm Detective Zenoni and this is Detective Wildow. We're here to ask you some questions concerning the murder of a student of yours, Tiffany Kehl."

"Oh, yes," he replied with a sigh, growing visibly calmer. "I heard about it on the news. I was waiting for someone to come speak with me. Please sit down."

Zenoni grabbed two uncomfortable metal chairs and sat them before Professor Mathis' desk. He felt like a high school student again since the classroom looked more like an eleventh-grade English class than an MBA lecture hall.

"When was the last time you saw Tiffany?" Zenoni asked, as Wildow prepared to take notes.

"Last week in class."

"Did anything seem to be bothering her? Was she acting unusual in any way?"

"No, I didn't see her behavior as being peculiar."

"What was she like?"

"The last time I saw her?"

"No, in general. Was she a good student? Was she active in class? What was she like to deal with on a regular basis?"

Edward Mathis sighed and drummed his fingers on his desk. "Tiffany wasn't easy to get along with. She was brilliant and the most driven person I'd ever met, but she was also opinionated and arrogant. She often disagreed with some of the business tactics I taught in class, and she wasn't shy about voicing her disapproval. I'll be honest, at times she intimidated me. She was persuasive and had a way of making people pay attention to her. On two occasions, she took over the class and gave much more zealous lectures than I ever could."

"It sounds like she got on your nerves."

"I worried about how she would affect my career. The students fill out a survey after every class and if they thought she was in more control than me, Lord knows what would happen. I *was* worried, especially with the recent budget cuts."

"Where were you last night?"

"I was at a teachers' conference. Then I went to the Bay View Diner, and after that, straight home. Surely you don't think I've done anything wrong! I would never do anything to harm a student."

"Do you know anyone who might have wanted to hurt Tiffany?"

"To be perfectly honest, I do know that she got into some

sort of altercation with another student. Apparently it was quite serious; I understand that Miss Kehl's car was damaged."

"Who was this other student?"

The professor's eyes shifted, "I don't know how ethical—"

"This is a murder investigation, Mr. Mathis," Wildow snapped.

"Olivia Larsen," the professor confessed.

"Do you know what the argument was about?"

"No. I haven't the slightest idea."

"When did it take place?"

"About three weeks ago, maybe a little less."

"We'll need to talk to Olivia," Zenoni replied.

Professor Mathis glanced at the clock. "She's due in my class tonight. If you're willing to wait a short time, I'm sure you'll be able to speak to her."

"Thank you. We'll do that."

Chapter Nine

Olivia Larsen had the kind of tough-as-nails, devil-may-care attitude that annoyed Zenoni immensely. A slight girl with shoulder-length black hair and impossibly pale skin, her skinny legs were clad in tight light-colored blue jeans. She wore a black T-shirt with an abundance of silver jewelry and thick leather boots. Leaning against the hallway wall like an indignant high school student, her silver lip ring gleaming in the overhead light, she seemed unfazed at being confronted by the two detectives.

"I have no reason to be nervous," she declared nonchalantly. "I didn't do anything wrong."

"No one's saying you did," Zenoni replied. "Do you know a Tiffany Kehl?"

For the first time Olivia looked alarmed. "Yeah, I do," she snapped. "Is that what this is about—the car? We worked that out privately, so why she would tell you about it now, I don't know. I—"

"Tiffany Kehl was found murdered in her place of employment yesterday morning."

"What?" Olivia asked, pushing herself away from the wall and standing before the detectives, rigid with alarm. She giggled nervously as her brown eyes darted between the two men. "Right before I came to class my boyfriend texted me about seeing some story in the paper about a dead classmate, but I

81

didn't have a chance to call him back. I thought he was kidding or at least mistaken."

"We heard you and Tiffany had an argument. What was it that you fought about?" Wildow asked directly.

"Nothing serious," Olivia declared, her voice rising with stress. "Nothing I'd kill her over."

"This is a murder investigation, Miss Larsen. Please answer the question."

Olivia cast her eyes down and shuffled her feet. It was an oddly childlike gesture. "Okay, I'll tell you. Tiffany was the golden girl of the class. She had this attitude like she was better than everyone else. It grated on my nerves. Anyway, one night we got into a debate about advertising techniques and she totally destroyed my point of view. It put me in a pretty bad mood, which only got worse when the professor asked me to stay after class to discuss my less-than-impressive grades. So, I finally get outside to meet my boyfriend, Donny, who was picking me up since my crappy car needed a battery change and was still in the garage. As soon as I got outside, I saw Tiffany chatting Donny up, and I just sort of snapped. I knew she had a weakness for men with money—she'd even joked about it in class—and Donny's parents are rich. He drives a new BMW and I knew she'd noticed that. I don't know, I was stressed, and I just freaked out and started yelling at her."

"What did she do?"

"She gave me a dirty look and walked away. But the following week, I had my car back, and I met Tiffany on the way to class. She could never leave anything alone. She mouthed off to me, asking how Donny was, in this real sharp tone of voice. I just went nuts. I waited until she went inside and then I walked over to her pretty red car and keyed it. Then I just walked into class like nothing happened. The security cameras caught me, though, so I ended up paying for the repairs, but at least she didn't call the police on me. I'm sorry I did it. I just flipped at the time."

"Okay," Zenoni replied, trying to sound nonjudgmental. "Did you learn much about Tiffany during your class time together?"

"Not at all. We tried to stay out of each other's way. I didn't like her, but I'm sorry she's dead."

"Where were you Monday night and early Tuesday morning?"

"I was out with Donny," she declared in an icy tone. "We went into the city since he had tickets for Smack Down Central."

"That's the big wrestling match, right?" Zenoni asked, recalling how he had seen the event advertised pretty much everywhere over the past few months. "Do you have any proof of your attendance?"

"Yeah," Olivia replied, reaching for her cell phone. "I took tons of pictures with this."

The battered cell phone's photos were far from top quality, but they clearly depicted images of Olivia and a tall sandy-haired young man standing in a large crowd. Below them, inside a center stage ring, one masked man was suspended in midair milliseconds away from pouncing on another spandex-clad man lying on the floor beneath him.

"What did you do after this event?"

"We had dinner at a burger joint and then we took the train home. We didn't get in until after three in the morning."

"Okay. Thank you, Miss Larsen," Zenoni declared, before asking if there was anything else she thought might be helpful to their investigation.

"No. Can I go now?"

Zenoni nodded and Olivia walked into her classroom, making sure to shut the door behind her with an audible click. Having exhausted that lead, the detectives made their way out of the building. Back in the car and heading toward the station, Wildow asked Zenoni what he thought of the unfolding case.

"Well, the professor had time to concoct a story since he knew about the murder. The girl seemed genuinely surprised, and her alibi was solid. I don't know yet. I'm still keeping every possibility open."

"We're on the same page then," Wildow replied, switching on the radio. Zenoni was happy to hear Eric Clapton wailing about "Layla." He needed something to keep him awake until he was able to go home and get some much-needed sleep.

Chapter Ten

There were snow flurries in the early hours of Thursday morning, making Zenoni's commute to work slower than usual. He was in his office less than ten minutes when Sandra burst into the room and announced that Alex Dedek, Tiffany's stalker boyfriend, had been located. She offered to have an officer pick him up and bring him to the station, but Zenoni thought that paying Alex a surprise visit at work would be more effective.

The Travest Computer Software Company was housed inside a large building covered entirely with blue glass that gleamed in the sunlight. The lobby was well furnished with marble tiles and abstract paintings; this establishment obviously did not suffer from the same financial burdens that The Treasure Chest Jewelry Television Studio did. The uniformed guard at the front desk was alarmed by the appearance of the detectives and insisted on informing Alex over the intercom that two men were on their way upstairs to see him.

When Zenoni and Wildow stepped off the elevator on the building's top floor, they were met by the stares of dozens of curious cubical workers. A tall, lanky man with a thick mop of black hair was standing outside a corner office with the word MANAGER printed on the door. He was leaning against a copy machine and eyeing the detectives suspiciously as they approached. Zenoni pulled out his badge, causing the man's eyes to grow wide. A number of audible gasps and snickers rang through the department.

"Alex Dedek, I'm Detective Zen—"

"Please step into my office!" the man hissed and quickly skirted into his private room. As soon as Wildow and Zenoni joined him, he slammed the door and drew the blinds. His eyes were darting frantically from one officer to the other, as if he were on the verge of a nervous breakdown.

"Why did you have to start showing your badges in front of *them*?" he exclaimed, pointing toward the door. "God only knows what they think now! They resent me like you wouldn't believe. Being thirty-three and having a doctorate in business means that I manage a lot of people nearly twice my age, and trust me, they don't like it one bit! They're always trying to find some way to get rid of me and mock me, and now they've got it! Why are you here anyway? I can assure you that all the funds are in order and—"

"We're here to discuss Tiffany Kehl," Zenoni replied, cutting Alex's tirade short. "You do know a Tiffany Kehl, don't you?"

"Of course I do. She's a good friend of mine," Alex replied, too surprised to continue his rant. "How do you know Tiffany? What has she got to do with police business?"

"Well—"

Before Zenoni could break the news, the copy machine outside the door started loudly. The noise jolted Alex, who immediately descended into another elaborate tangent.

"They're listening in!" he declared dramatically. "We can't talk here! I'll take an early lunch so we can discuss this matter. I cannot have a proper conversation with the minions around!"

Minions? How did Tiffany ever see anything in this guy? Zenoni thought, as he shot the equally shocked Wildow a quick smirk and followed Alex out of the office.

* * *

Ten minutes later, Alex and the detectives sat in a secluded section of the food court on the ground floor of the spacious office building. Like the rest of the building, it was finely furnished, but also decorated with an abundance of potted plants. Light music radiated gently from overhead speakers. Zenoni and Wildow had cups of coffee while Alex got himself a coffee and a chicken Caesar salad. He had just swallowed his first bite of salad and taken his second gulp of coffee when Zenoni broke the news of Tiffany's death.

"That's not possible!" he stuttered in response, his eyes wide and glassy.

"I'm afraid it's been confirmed."

"How?" he asked in a shocked voice, his hands shaking and his jaw trembling.

"She was beaten to death, murdered."

Alex looked utterly stunned.

"The story was all over the local news and papers yesterday and today. Did you really have no inkling of what happened?" Wildow asked, obviously skeptical.

Alex shook his head vigorously. "I don't watch the news much and I haven't had a chance to read the paper recently. I didn't see anything—I didn't know . . . It doesn't seem possible." He put his head in his hands and let out a deeply tormented sigh.

"How well did you know Tiffany?" Zenoni asked.

"She was the light of my life. We met three months ago at a nightclub. I don't usually attend such places, but it was fate that led me to her there. She was perfect."

"Some people have suggested that Tiffany thought you were stalking her," Wildow replied matter-of-factly.

Alex looked up quickly. "No, no, no," he replied, giggling nervously. "We loved each other. We had a special and intense connection."

"And she thought so too?"

"Of course she did!"

"When was the last time you saw Tiffany?"

"Saturday night. We had dinner."

"That's interesting because, according to our records, Tiffany was working all Saturday."

"Well . . . I . . . I just can't believe she's gone! I just don't understand how this could have happened to her!" Alex's voice broke off into a sob, which he muted by burying his face in his hands once again. Wiping his tearing eyes, he asked to use the bathroom. "I don't want to be seen in this condition. I need to compose myself," he exclaimed as he stood up awkwardly and sprinted toward the bathroom.

Zenoni followed him into the men's room and stood by the sinks waiting for Alex to come out of the stall. He didn't like leaving possible suspects alone. Suddenly the sound of a window opening filled the air. *He's escaping,* Zenoni thought quickly, as he kicked open the stall door just in time to see Alex, who had jumped out of the bathroom window, running across the parking lot with his car keys in hand. Feeling like an idiot for not checking the stall for windows, Zenoni raced out of the men's room.

"Nolan, he's gone!" he shouted, running through the cafeteria at top speed, causing other lunch-goers to look up from their meals in shock. Without missing a beat, Wildow jumped up and followed Zenoni out of the building.

By the time Zenoni started up the unmarked car, Alex was already peeling out of the lot in his dark blue Cadillac Seville. Zenoni turned on the dashboard-mounted flashing lights and floored the engine. Beside him Wildow radioed for backup. Zenoni had been trained to handle high-speed chases, but it had been years since he needed to use the skills, and they had grown dull after such a long period of inactivity. The icy road conditions only increased the chaos when Alex turned onto the highway.

It was midday and traffic was moving along nicely, enabling Alex to dramatically increase his speed. He zipped in and out of lanes, dodging other cars by mere inches and frightening other drivers into swerving. One compact green car with a BABY-ON-BOARD sign in the back window avoided crashing into Alex's Cadillac by half an inch. The surprised driver slammed on the brakes and blew the horn loudly. Undaunted, Alex pressed harder on the accelerator and tailgated a large red pickup truck for a few moments before sharply veering into the left lane, barely avoiding the grille of an aging white van.

For Zenoni, time was in overdrive. He heard the blaring of horns distantly and saw the painted white lines on the road zipping past, as he remained focused on keeping pace with Alex. Then the sirens of patrol cars filled the air and three marked police vehicles passed him. Zenoni kept his speed even, but remained at a distance as the police units closed in on the suspect. Alex was obviously shaken by the number of police cars after him. His steering was becoming increasingly erratic. The large Cadillac was shaking in the lane, veering drastically from one side of the road to the other while increasing speed, making it difficult for the patrol cars to catch up.

The chase lasted for ten minutes, which seemed like ten hours. Zenoni was starting to think they would chase Alex until they ran out of gas when Alex finally lost control in the slippery conditions, spun off the highway, and crashed his luxury car into the woods by the side of the highway. The shattering of glass and crunch of metal resounded for miles. Incredibly, Alex still refused to surrender. His right leg was bloody and he appeared to be in pain, yet he still managed to swing the driver's side door open and lurch into the foliage. The police were right behind him; they quickly pulled onto the side of the road and stopped dead a few feet away from his flaming vehicle. One of the cars was a K-9 unit, and the officer released a barking German shepherd to chase Alex. The dog followed its orders well, and as Zenoni and Wildow pulled onto the side of the road, the canine had Alex by the arm and was shaking him from side to side as if he was a chew toy. Alex was screaming and trying to get the dog away from him by beating its ears and head. His antics only increased the dog's aggressiveness, and it shook Alex harder and harder until he lost his balance and slipped deeper into the woods—the German shepherd behind him. The K-9 unit officer ran toward the trees shouting commands at his four-legged partner in German. Not wanting to miss the action, Wildow and Zenoni got out of their car and raced to the woods. When they got there, the German shepherd was sitting beside the K-9 unit officer, looking as docile as a lamb. Alex was lying on the snowy grass holding his bleeding leg and howling in agony.

"It's broken!" he shrieked. "That dog made me break my leg! I'll have you all sued for police brutality!"

"Oh yeah?" the K-9 officer replied casually. "You were resisting arrest, and we have camera footage from the cars to prove it. You've done this entirely to yourself, buddy."

Within a few minutes an ambulance arrived. Alex was read his Miranda rights and placed under arrest as he was lifted onto a stretcher by a team of paramedics. Despite his pain, or maybe because of it, Alex had lost all sense of composure and was spewing colorful profanities at the police. Although he was unresponsive to his suspect's foul-mouthed tirade, mentally Zenoni listed all the questions he had for Alex as he and Wildow followed the ambulance to the hospital in their car. He was anticipating finding out the truth about Alex's relationship with Tiffany once he was able to subject the squirrelly executive to some serious questioning.

Chapter Eleven

The doctors at the Mother of Mercy Medical Center's emergency room claimed that Alex's leg was broken in three places and needed to be operated on immediately. As Alex went under the knife, the detectives went to court and secured a warrant to search his home—a sprawling three-story mini-mansion.

If Tiffany had liked men with cash, Alex surely seemed like a prime candidate. Everything inside his enormous redbrick, colonial-style home reeked of money. It took the detectives over an hour to search the house. Like Tiffany, Alex enjoyed the finer things in life—every gadget and gizmo was brand-new and of prime technology. Everything appeared to be in order until they walked into the bedroom closet and found the shrine. Alex's large walk-in closet was the size of Zenoni's bathroom. Standing on the center shelf on the back wall was a massive collage of photos of Tiffany pasted to a gigantic white board.

"For someone who only dated the girl for three months, he sure took a lot of pictures of her," Zenoni declared.

"Some of these look like she didn't know she was being photographed," Wildow remarked.

"You just read my mind," Zenoni replied, staring at the various photos of Tiffany coming in and out of her car, shopping, and walking her dog. "Do you suppose that he followed her around to take these? Like maybe he just stayed in his car and clicked away?"

Wildow nodded. "That's exactly what I think happened. The guy's a class-A creep and I wouldn't put much past him. There's got to be close to four hundred pictures here! Can you imagine the amount of time he spent taking them, printing them, cutting them out, and pasting them here? It's a wonder he got any work done at the office."

"Who knows, maybe he took them to work and this is what he did all day with his door closed and the blinds drawn," Zenoni replied. How Alex had managed to stalk Tiffany and still have time for his job was beyond comprehension. "Multitasking must be his strong point," Zenoni mused as he pried the picture-covered board off the wall. "I'm collecting this as evidence. I'm pretty interested to hear the story he tells about it."

As soon as the board was liberated from the wall, the detectives walked downstairs and left the house. Seated in the passenger side of the car, Wildow looked out at the lavish house and sighed.

"What?" Zenoni asked, hoping that nothing had been forgotten inside.

"I was just thinking about how strange the world is. Here we have this young guy who's got the highest degree, a great job with an enormous salary, a huge house, and money to burn, yet he's one of the biggest weirdos I've ever come across."

Zenoni smirked as he started up the engine. "You're right," he agreed, backing out of the parking lot, "and now this privileged weirdo has got some serious explaining to do."

Alex was out of surgery by the time the detectives got back to the hospital. Although he was still woozy from the anesthetic, he was coherent enough to be interviewed. To ensure no further incident with him, he had been handcuffed to the bed. A uniformed officer was standing guard looking both bored and peeved by Alex's ceaseless whining.

"Not you again," Alex wailed when he saw the detectives. "I'll call both my nurse and my attorney!"

At least he's not cussing us out, Zenoni thought, grateful for any small decency he was given.

"We have to interview you sooner or later," Wildow replied coolly. "And, if you really didn't have anything to do with Tiffany's death, talking to us now will look a lot better on your record than having your lawyer called."

Alex didn't respond, but he didn't protest either. Zenoni pulled out a small tape recorder and pressed down the red RECORD button to save the interview as part of his official report. Then he jumped into the questioning. "Tell us about your relationship with Tiffany."

"She was the most amazing person I ever met," Alex explained.

"Is that why you made a hidden shrine to her?"

"I loved her. We belonged together."

"Not according to what we've been hearing. We were told that Tiffany was seen squabbling with you outside the television studio. Is that true?"

"All lovers quarrel from time to time."

"We heard she was threatening to get a restraining order."

"She was in denial about our love."

"Why did you lie to us about the last time you saw Tiffany?"

"I told you, I was in shock and confused."

"I don't believe that's the only reason."

"That's too bad, because I'm telling the truth."

"The woman was afraid of you, Alex!" Wildow shouted suddenly. "She wanted to get a restraining order against you! Doesn't that send a clear message? She told you point-blank that she wanted you to leave her alone, but you just wouldn't get the message. We were at your house and we found all those pictures you took while you stalked her. I'll tell you straight up, things don't look too good for you at the moment, and I think you better start talking to us. Now, I'm going to ask you this once and, for your own sake, you better be honest with me: Where were you late Monday night?"

Wildow's cold eyes bored into Alex, who was unable to maintain the gaze.

"I have no idea what happened," he wailed. "We were so happy together and then she just got cold toward me. When I questioned her about her attitude, she said I was too clingy. I thought she was just confused—love can do that to people— but she never warmed to me again, and the more I tried to reason with her the more distant she became. She said she didn't want anything serious and I felt rejected. I didn't know how to handle the situation. I mean, the only time I got to see her was when she was on television. Can you imagine that? I loved her and yet I was reduced to watching her as I sat at home like one of her shoppers! I couldn't get her out of my head, and for the past few days, Monday included, I went to the mall after work and roamed around the jewelry stores. They made me remember the good times with Tiffany."

"What time was this?"

"I was in the mall for about four hours—it was about to close when I left. So I guess I was there from roughly six to ten P.M."

"What did you do after you left the mall?"

"I went home."

"Straight home?"

"Pretty much," Alex replied, twiddling his thumbs nervously.

"Do I have to remind you again that this is a murder investigation and withholding evidence is unlawful?"

"Okay, okay. I went to get something to eat at the Gossip

Diner. I was there until about eleven. Then I went to see a movie."

"Where?"

"In the city. Southern Queens to be exact."

"Which theater, what movie?"

"The Burlesque Theater; *Love Handles* was the film."

Unable to help himself, Zenoni raised his eyebrows in an expression of surprised amusement. Alex wasn't the sort of man he would have guessed to attend dirty movies.

"Don't tell anyone!" Alex pleaded, "Oh please, don't let anyone know I was there! I'll never get over the humiliation! I'd rather be taken out and shot than have this made public!"

"Relax, Mr. Dedek. I'm not going to tell on you," Zenoni reassured him. "I'm just amazed by what I'm hearing. You're telling me that you went through all of this—running from the police, a car accident, a broken leg—just to avoid admitting you went to see an adult film?"

Alex nodded.

Zenoni shook his head in an expression of pure disbelief. "What time were you there until?"

"It ended at around three in the morning. I had to drive home and I didn't get in the door of my house until a few minutes after four."

"Wait," Wildow cut in, "the movie ended at three? So if you got there around midnight that means you were gone for four hours?"

"It was a double feature: *Love Handles* one and two," Alex squeaked.

"So if we check the theater's security cameras you're sure you'll be on them?"

"Yes," Alex sobbed, more humiliated than ever. "I'm so alone now that my Tiffany's gone!"

He broke down completely as Zenoni declared the interview

over and pressed the STOP button on his recorder. He allowed Alex a few moments to gain control over himself before informing the flabbergasted man that he was being charged with resisting arrest, endangerment of others, and various traffic violations due to his getaway attempt. Leaving Alex to mull over the bad turn his life had taken, the detectives made their way out of the hospital.

"Unbelievable," Wildow muttered as he got off the elevator. "All of that to hide a fact we would have uncovered anyway."

"We'll have his story checked out first thing in the morning," Zenoni replied as he and his partner walked down the hospital's brightly decorated main corridor. The detectives had barely stepped outside the hospital when the bright lights of flashing cameras assaulted them. Before he had time to register what was happening, a microphone was shoved under Zenoni's nose.

"What can you tell us about the case?" a perky yet pushy voice demanded to know. Zenoni knew the slender young woman with the short brown hair who was standing in front of him: Melody Zielinski, an infamously aggressive local reporter.

"No comment," Zenoni replied. He was all too aware of the rolling camera behind him as he pushed away the large microphone embedded with the news station logo.

"Is it true your suspect previously dated the victim?" Melody persisted.

"No comment!" Zenoni repeated, anger slicing his words. If Melody had any other questions, she didn't have a chance to ask them before the detectives reached their car and quickly drove away from the hospital.

Sandra ran to the detectives as soon as they got back to the station. "What happened?" she asked, her eyes wide with shocked curiosity. "That big chase is all over the news. Someone leaked Alex's name and now this Melody Zielinski woman is reporting that he was Tiffany's boyfriend. Apparently some people from his office were more than willing to talk to the reporters. The whole thing has the big suits over in Town Hall hysterical. Sergeant Veglak has been on the phone with them all morning."

Zenoni sighed audibly. Veglak would not be pleased about this. Zenoni could almost hear his Slavic voice shouting about the detectives' carelessness.

I was careless, Zenoni thought sadly, *and now the politicians are panicking about the possibility of this incident tarnishing the town's reputation.*

"It's been such a hard morning—is there any good news at all?" Zenoni asked in desperation.

To his surprise, Sandra nodded. "Security cameras confirmed Edward Mathis' story. He was at a teachers' conference and then at a diner on the night Tiffany was killed. So that's another suspect off the list."

"Well, there's something positive," Zenoni replied and walked into his office.

"Are you okay?" Wildow asked as Zenoni slouched down into his chair and rubbed his eyes.

"Not really. This whole media/political mess is because of me. I should have checked the bathroom stall first. I let him get away."

Wildow shrugged. "He wasn't under arrest or anything, and he did scoot in there before we had a chance to react. It was unexpected and it wasn't entirely your fault. He escaped. You did follow him; and the second you realized he was making a run for it, you pursued him. We got the guy and we got a statement; that's the bottom line. Who knows, maybe if he hadn't been sent to the hospital after that whole ordeal we wouldn't have gotten him to talk. The guy was a pretty hard egg to crack."

Wildow's words were truthful and his voice was comforting,

but the pit in Zenoni's stomach lingered. Suddenly Sandra appeared in the doorway, staring at Zenoni.

"Your wife's on the phone. She said she was trying to call you, but your cell phone's not working."

"That's because the signal dies in the hospital," Zenoni replied, leaning forward in his chair to pick up the phone. "Is she on line one?" Sandra nodded and Zenoni thanked her before he placed the receiver to his ear and greeted his wife.

"Finally I got ahold of you! I've been calling all afternoon! From now on you really have to check to make sure your cell is on," Lorraine scolded, sounding flustered. "I'm at the storage place getting the decorations out. Now, I've got the elves' Ferris wheel loaded into the car. I'm thinking of coming back for the carousel, but I don't want to make the extra trip unless it's for a reason, so if I bring it home will you promise to install it as soon as you can—tonight maybe?"

She said more, but Zenoni didn't hear her. He was in no mood to discuss the placement of Christmas ornaments.

"I'm not promising anything, Lorraine!" he shouted. "I'm having a heck of a day at work—turn the news on if you want proof—and I'm not thinking about decorating right now! You can do it yourself if you want, but don't break my chops about it again!"

With that said he slammed the phone into its cradle. Even before he let go of the handles he regretted his harsh words. *This job's gonna drive me crazy,* he thought, once again envisioning retirement.

Chapter Twelve

That night, on his way home from work, Angelo Zenoni picked up dinner at a local Italian restaurant and drove it to the Rose-View Senior Care Center where his mother resided. His day had been bad, but not as rough as expected. Sergeant Veglak had come by the office questioning the sequence of events that had unfolded, barely holding his temper. Yet after hearing the full story, he visibly cooled down, realizing that it had been handled to the best of the detectives' ability. Zenoni had not been thrown off the case or written up, so he supposed things could have been much worse.

Zenoni parked and stepped out of his car. It was dark, and above the glare of the streetlights, hundreds of white stars glimmered in the velvet-black sky. Although the night was beautiful, it was also cold, and Zenoni was happy to step inside the senior center's cozy lobby. He smiled at Courtney, one of the nurses who worked at the reception area, and proceeded to the elevator.

The building had three stories and Zenoni had made sure to secure his mother a room on the top floor so no footfalls from upstairs neighbors would annoy her. Zenoni entered his mother's room to find her sitting in her favorite chair, watching programs on the Game Show Network. Although she was eighty-nine years of age, Viviane Zenoni's mind was sharp and she enjoyed guessing game-show trivia. She had mastered text messaging on her cell phone and she often stayed up late into the night texting into live interactive game shows. Twice she had won a prize—a coffee mug and a hat—quickly gaining a place of honor on the top shelf of her wall unit.

"Neglecting your firstborn for game shows, huh?" Zenoni joked as he set the food down on a table and planted a kiss on his mother's cheek.

"She's used up all her lifelines; she'll never make it to a million," Viviane declared while staring at the television where a woman was breathing a sigh of relief after winning sixty-four thousand dollars on *Who Wants to be a Millionaire?*

She has no idea what's coming her way this Christmas, Zenoni thought, eyeing his mother's aging twenty-four-inch TV. He and Lorraine had purchased a forty-eight-inch flat-screen HDTV for her that they would give her as a gift on Christmas day.

Smiling, Viviane kissed her son's cheek and muted the program. "What did you bring for supper?" she asked, rising from her comfy recliner.

"Chicken parmigiana, your favorite."

"You're a good son," Viviane replied, smiling as she carried the food into the small kitchenette. "Your father would be proud." At the mention of her late husband, Viviane grew quiet. Rick Zenoni had died peacefully in his sleep two years before, at the age of ninety-four. "How's Lorraine?" she asked to lighten the mood.

"She's fine. We're in the process of Christmas decorating."

"I'm sure Alexis' girls will be enthralled, as always."

Zenoni smiled thinking of his eight- and ten-year-old nieces, Adrianna and Brianna, and their delighted reaction to his decorations. Every Christmas he invited his sister, Alexis, her husband, John, and their two girls over for dinner.

"Are Lorraine's parents coming from Florida?" Viviane questioned.

"They'll be here on the twenty-first of December."

"Are you picking them up at the airport?"

"Yup."

"Good. You know how cabbies cheat tourists." Zenoni simply nodded. For as long as he could remember his mother had distrusted yellow cabs. "How's Denise?" she asked.

"She's good. She'll be over on Christmas too."

"And her son? I remember when he was little, he drew me a picture of his house—such a sweet little boy! I was so sorry for him when his father died, as if fourteen isn't a hard enough age! Is he doing well?"

"Yeah, he's fine," Zenoni lied. He assumed his mother would have a heart attack if she saw the way Denise's "sweet little boy" had turned out.

"And how are you?" she asked, turning to look at her son with her hands on her hips.

"I'm good, Mama," he replied the same way he had when he was a child.

Viviane wasn't convinced. "Something's bothering you. I can always tell. What happened?"

Zenoni knew that if he didn't confess his worries, his mother would spend the remainder of the evening attempting to pry them out of him. It was easier to come clean, and so he spent the next fifteen minutes recapping the Alex Dedek–escape disaster to his mother. "I screwed up, Mama, really bad, and because of me the whole thing's on the news."

"Well, you got the guy and didn't get hurt. Your boss seemed understanding too, so it wasn't that bad. You're too hard on yourself. Have some spaghetti. I can't eat all of this, and a full stomach will make you feel better."

"I also yelled at Lorraine," Zenoni admitted, as he dug into the plate of spaghetti his mother had set in front of him.

"Why?"

"She called right after I got into the station and was carrying on about decorating. I was under stress and I just lost it. I didn't mean to."

"I'm sure she'll forgive you. She's put up with worse with the crazy hours you work. My advice is to repent by decorating every spare chance you get. At least Lorraine is helping you with the ornaments; give her a kiss for that! My Aunt Annie never even put a bulb on the tree for my Uncle Giuseppe. She had him up on the ladder hanging lights on the roof even when he had a broken leg!"

"I'll decorate as soon as I can. Lorraine knows that," Zenoni replied. "We've got some great new lawn ornaments this year: Santa and Frosty the Snowman in a hot air balloon. It actually hovers in the air."

"They get better and better," Viviane agreed as she sat down to her meal. "Remember the first time we put those circling ornaments on the tree, the ones with the little motors in them?"

"Yeah. They got wrapped in the branches and short-circuited the blinking string of lights. Papa yelled himself hoarse untangling that whole mess," Zenoni recalled as he laughed at the memory.

For the next half hour Zenoni and his mother ate and reminisced about decorating in years past. By the time he kissed his mother goodnight and walked back to his car, Zenoni was anticipating the coming season. *It's funny how an hour with Mama can make me want to start setting up the house for the holidays,* he thought, smiling as he started up the car and drove home with Billy Joel proclaiming that he was in a "New York State of Mind." *Maybe I will hang some lights on the living room windows tonight. I'll call it an early Christmas present for Lorraine.*

Chapter Thirteen

Zenoni got into his office on Friday morning with a sore back and aching fingers. He had been up late the previous night hanging lights on windows, and although his eyelids were heavy, his conscience was clear: Lorraine had jumped for joy when she woke and saw what he had done. He barely had time to take a first sip of coffee when Sandra approached him with a wide smile on her face.

"Alex Dedek's alibi was confirmed this morning. Security cameras at the theater place him there at the time of the murder, so he's off the list of suspects for sure. Now for the big news—we tracked down Christina, Tiffany's sister."

Christina Kehl was living in a Brooklyn homeless shelter run by a church charity organization. She was located when she contacted the authorities of her own accord after seeing the news of her sister's death on TV. The police took her information over the phone and passed it along to Zenoni's station. Christina wanted the police to come and speak with her; Zenoni and Wildow were happy to comply.

They were on their way to Brooklyn a half an hour after being informed of her discovery. Traffic was bad; the homeless shelter was worse. It was housed inside a small, square, graffiti-covered, one-story concrete building, jammed between a furniture factory and an abandoned warehouse, in the kind of neighborhood Zenoni wouldn't want to walk around in at night or even leave his car parked in during the day. When he had worked homicide in the city, he became well acquainted with this hard-luck neighborhood, where trouble was always a few steps away.

The inside of the shelter was drab and reeked of desperation. The poor economy had obviously put a heavy financial strain on the institution. The ultrabright fluorescent lights only highlighted the dusty windows and dirty floor. Despite the bleak conditions, the girl at the front desk was friendly. The shelter was much bigger than Zenoni had thought; the staff girl led them down a seemingly endless corridor before turning into a sprawling dining area filled with countless rows of rickety tables and chairs and the smell of poorly prepared food. The walls were painted an unfortunate shade of mustard yellow that, Zenoni supposed, was meant to be cheerful. The laminated-tile floor was cracking and gave a small squeak every time a foot fell upon it. The room was inhabited by dozens of down-on-their-luck individuals, most of whom had long dirty hair and tattered clothing, and looked as if they'd been acquainted with street life for some time. Zenoni had to admit to himself that he was comforted by the presence of his gun, considering the sneers and distrustful glances he was receiving from a substantial number of the shelter's less-than-savory characters. The staff girl stopped, pointed to a table toward the back of the room, gave the detectives a wan smile, and proceeded back to her post at the front desk.

A tall, skinny woman was sitting alone at the table in the back right corner of the dining room, fiddling with a white Styrofoam cup held in her slender hands. Her jet-black hair was in stark contrast to her incredibly pale skin. At first Zenoni thought Christina looked like a teenager, but as he approached her, he was surprised by how old she looked. Her face was deeply set with lines, aging her well past her thirty years. She wore a thin cotton shirt with the HARLEY DAVIDSON logo printed on it. Although the cloth might once have been black, numerous washings had left it a dull gray.

"Christina Kehl?" Zenoni asked, with his badge out.

The woman looked up at him with hard yet wounded eyes. "Call me Christie; and my last name's Norrah, not Kehl. Tommy Kehl's nothing but my stepfather. My real father's last name is Norrah."

"Well, I'm glad you contacted us, Christie Norrah," Zenoni replied. "We were having a hard time tracking you."

"So you actually knew about me, huh?" Christie asked in faux surprise, a small and resentful smile forming on her lips.

"Some acquaintances of your sister knew of you, yes."

Christie uttered a short and embittered laugh. "It's good to know she let some people know of my existence, so I wasn't just a dirty little secret in her otherwise bright life. Anyway, believe it or not, she was actually pretty nice to me, which is incredible given who she was raised by."

"When did you become aware of her death?" Wildow asked, ready to take notes.

Christie's attitude softened at the question. "Last night on the news. I couldn't believe it. I broke down crying right in the middle of the common room. I think I scared the other people around me half to death."

"I'm sorry for your loss," Zenoni replied sincerely, "but I really would appreciate it if you could tell us about your relationship with your sister."

"She was really my half-sister," Christie explained, staring down at the table to hide her tearing eyes. "She was my mom's kid with my stepfather, and she was the light of their lives. In their eyes, she was Jekyll and I was Hyde. Every time something went wrong, I got the blame. Tiffany never did because they considered her perfect. Here's the funny thing though: she never bought into all the favoritism. As we got older, I think she was ashamed of how the folks treated me. Maybe that's why she tried to be so nice as an adult—I don't know. Anyway, we had some good times as kids. We used to explore the woods behind the house together. We actually had fun, bonding and all, you know? Then one day when she was seven, we were playing by the creek, and she fell off a log and cut her left ankle on a branch. The folks freaked out and blamed me even though she tried to defend me. We never were allowed to play near there again. Actually, after that, they wanted to keep her away from me, always thinking I'd get her in trouble. She wasn't a bad kid, though. Even as the ultra-driven, good-looking, style-smart business woman she turned out to be, she never blamed me for the mark that incident left."

Zenoni nodded, remembering the scar Zhang had pointed out on Tiffany's left ankle; there was one mystery solved.

"Anyway," Christie continued, "as we got older, things between me and the Kehls got worse. I wasn't good in school, they didn't like the way I dressed, I didn't have adequate long-term goals, blah, blah, blah. They drove me nuts. The day I turned eighteen, they kicked me out and I left gladly. I never finished high school or anything. I moved over here since I knew some people who were into the whole art scene, you know? It was cool. I asked Tiffany to come hang out, but she wouldn't take me up on the offer. She never liked my friends. She did come to see me once a month though, and she always brought extra food and clothes and stuff, even though I never asked her to. She did all this behind the Kehls' backs. As far as they were concerned, I had been disowned by everyone."

"When was the last time you saw Tiffany?" Zenoni asked gently, aware of the way Christie's words were catching in her throat.

"Last month was the last time I actually saw her, but I spoke to her on Friday afternoon. It wasn't the nicest of conversations either."

"Can you elaborate on that?" Wildow pressed.

Christie took a deep breath. "I had this boyfriend, Dominick. He's a musician and he did the whole starving-artist thing, even though he had an apartment and all. I didn't have anywhere else to go so I used to crash at his place. He was really moody, though. On Thursday, I ate a yogurt I found in the fridge. Well, Dominick freaked out when he realized I'd eaten the last yogurt, and he went into this tangent about how he didn't have money for nothing else, and I could have at least shared it, and all this other nonsense. I don't like being yelled at, and I started screaming right back at him. Before I know it, he's telling me to get out or he's calling the police to take me out. So, I got a few things together and went. Kicked out over yogurt—how's that for stupid?

"Anyway, I got outside and realized I had nowhere to go, since my painting career hasn't taken off yet and I have no money. I didn't want to sleep under a bridge, so I called Tiffany from a pay phone that I was lucky enough to find change in. I figured she'd help me out. She had enough dough to go around—part of it from her job, and most of it because the Kehls gave her anything she wanted. They brought her that pretty red car and the down payment on her house, so she had more money for shoes and clothes, you know. Anyway, when I called her and told her what happened, she just flipped. She refused to give me anything, since she thought I was in one of my downer moods and would only use it to buy drugs. I kinda had a problem in the past, you know?"

Zenoni nodded. Every time Christie moved her lips, he saw her badly decayed teeth—a telltale sign of a drug addict.

"Anyway, I started yelling at her and she told me she was going to call the cops and tell them about my habits. I cussed her out and hung up. That's the last time I ever spoke to her. I wish I hadn't gotten mad like that. She was good to me. Right before we had that fight, she told me she had some coats and blankets she was going to bring to me."

That explains the coats in the trunk, Zenoni thought, remembering the mountain of winter attire in Tiffany's car.

"What happened after you fought with her on the phone?" Wildow demanded to know.

"I came here. I'd seen this place advertised, and I figured I had nothing to lose; it's better than sleeping on the streets. I've been here since Friday night and haven't left once. You can check with any of the staff and they'll confirm it. Look, I've done bad stuff and I've screwed up my life, and I've only stayed out of jail due to pure luck, but I would never have hurt my sister. She was the only person in the world who actually cared about me. She could be vapid and annoying, but I never had any reason to kill her."

"Okay, but do you have any information you think might be helpful to us?" Zenoni asked. "Did you ever see her arguing with anyone? Did she ever mention someone giving her trouble?"

Christie nodded. "That's why I wanted to talk to you guys. Me and her weren't exactly close—we didn't confide deep secrets or anything—so I didn't know much about her personal life, but I did hear her fighting on her cell phone with this guy Arnold a few times. They were pretty nasty arguments."

"Any idea what they were about?"

Christie shook her head. "I have no clue. She tried not to argue too much in front of me. She did mention that the guy was her idiot boss. The last time I saw her she was fighting with him on her cell again, ranting and raving about how he couldn't force her out of the job, and she had dirt on him, and on and on. I don't think I'd ever heard her scream like that."

"So she thought Arnold was trying to push her out of her job?"

Christie nodded. "That's what she was saying. She kept telling him that she had dirt on him, and if he tried to do anything to her career, she would see to it that his was finished forever."

"Did she ever say what kind of dirt she had on him?"

Christie shook her head.

"And this happened the last time you saw her, a month ago—so late October, right?"

"Yeah, it was right before Halloween."

"Anything else you'd like to add?"

"No," Christie replied drearily. "I just wish our last conversation hadn't consisted of screeching insults. I loved her despite all the problems growing up. She was younger than me, but she was bright, and always trying to get me to improve myself. I guess I owe it to her to stay here and try to clean my act up a little. It's not the Ritz, but it's better than living homeless until overdosing."

"You've been very helpful and I thank you for taking the time to contact us and talk to us," Zenoni declared, as he rose from the rickety seat he had taken. "Again, I'm sorry for your loss, and please don't hesitate to call if you think of anything else."

Christie nodded. "I will. I'll be here for a while, so when you catch the person who did it, will you call the shelter and let me know?"

"That's a deal."

"Tiffany was a good person; she didn't deserve to die like that."

"I promise you, whoever did this is going to go to jail for a long time. We'll notify you if there's a break in the case. Take care of yourself, okay?"

Christie nodded and gave another wan smile, despite the fact that tears were falling freely from her eyes. After briefly talking to the staff, Zenoni was happy to get out of the dreary shelter and into his cozy vehicle.

"At least the car wasn't dismembered in any way," Wildow mused, considering the area they were in. "That's a big plus."

Zenoni nodded and started the engine. "What did you think of the sister?"

Wildow made a *tsk* sound. "That one has seen some hard times, but I don't think she's lying. She seemed genuinely upset about the death and *she* contacted *us*. Why do that if she has something to hide? Plus, she's an addict. I think it's safe to say that if she was responsible for this, any jewels or money would have been taken from the scene to support her habit."

"I agree. Tiffany was the only person who showed her sister any sort of compassion. I can't see Christie doing this, and her alibi is solid. According to the staff, she was there on the night of the murder."

"Slowly it's narrowing down."

"Yeah, but it's not making any more sense. I don't know, right now I just want to get back to the station and get Arnold Genson into the interview room as soon as possible."

Traffic was heavy on the way back to Long Island. The setting sun was casting a fiery reddish orange glow along the skyline by the time Zenoni pulled into the headquarters parking lot. As soon as he walked through the doors of the station, he requested that Sandra contact Arnold Genson.

"So how's the decorating going?" Wildow asked Zenoni as he approached the coffee machine in the break room.

"Don't even get me started," Zenoni groaned.

"That bad, huh?"

"If I see one more image of Saint Nick, I'll crack up."

"It's a real chore all right," Wildow agreed, handing Zenoni a paper cup full of decaffeinated coffee.

Zenoni agreed, as he took his first sip of the steamy brew. "It's never ending. The tree, the window lights, the ornaments, the porcelain village—it just goes on and on! And the lawn decorations are the worst part. I'm up on my roof in sixteen-degree weather securing a lighted plastic sculpture of Santa, his sled, and twelve reindeer; that can't be the action of a sane man." Suddenly his stomach lurched, the acid from his ulcer rising into a reflux that made him cringe in pain.

"Are you all right?" Wildow asked, concern lacing his words.

"Yeah. I can't shake the effects of this ulcer."

"Maybe you should go to a doctor and have it looked at, just to make sure it's not getting more serious." Wildow's tone was pleasant, but he was looking at Zenoni solemnly. They had become friends over the years since they worked their first case together—the shooting death of an ice cream man orchestrated by a competitor over their selling routes—and Zenoni knew Wildow was genuinely concerned for him.

"It's gotten better than it was, but I'll get it checked out by a doctor if it's still flaring up after the holidays."

"This time of year doesn't do much for a nervous condition, in my opinion," Wildow lamented. "I don't know about you, but the holidays always stress me out. Between Betty and her sister Beatrice, I know I'm bound to hear about every disease and every possible food fatality on the planet. Last year Betty insisted on cutting my turkey dinner into little slivers because she thought I was going to choke to death on a bone or—worse—eat too fast and get indigestion or some sort of kidney stone. That led to a whole conversation about operations and all the things doctors could do wrong resulting in complications. Trust me, it's not easy trying to enjoy eggnog over that."

"I'd believe it," Zenoni replied, suppressing a laugh with difficulty. Had Sandra not entered the room at that moment, his amusement would have been apparent.

"I called the jewelry studio and Genson isn't there," Sandra declared. "The receptionist, a woman named Bridget, told me that Genson took the day off to go fishing."

"Do you know which port or boat name?" Zenoni asked.

"No. And I called his house; there was no answer."

"We need to speak with him pronto, even if that means pulling the boat back to port, and we can't do that if we don't know the name or the dock."

"Well, I asked," Sandra replied in her own defense. "The girl didn't know."

"We told him not to leave until the investigation was over."

"He didn't leave the country. I was told he's expected back at work at nine A.M. tomorrow."

Frustration washed over Zenoni. He wanted to get this lead out of the way; having to wait until morning was irksome.

"Why not just wait until tomorrow?" Wildow asked. "We could go check his house, but it would most likely be a waste of time; we have no basis to search it, and if he's not there, or is just hiding out, we have no right to enter it. We'll deal with him in the morning when he comes back from his fishing trip. Is everything else settled for now?"

"I think we've done all we can for the time being," Zenoni replied. "All reports are filed, and aside from Genson, there are no new leads."

"Why don't you two take an early leave tonight?" Sandra

suggested. "You'll be working all day tomorrow, so I bet your wives will like having you home early today."

Zenoni rolled his eyes sarcastically at his smirking secretary. "I know what you're thinking. The old boss will end up setting up Santas until he drops. Ha-ha, very amusing."

Yet, because there was nothing more to do on the job, Zenoni took Sandra's advice and called it an early evening. At least he wasn't likely to hear the horrors of food-related deaths as he draped the tree in twinkling lights.

Chapter Fourteen

Lorraine was surprised and pleased to see her husband home so early and she celebrated the occasion by promptly putting him to work assembling the final touches on the artificial Christmas tree.

"After you've got the branches sorted out, you might want to take a look at the lights; those strings seemed awfully knotted to me when I peeked in the box," she stated cheerfully, perched atop a ladder hanging tinsel around the top of the wall unit.

"Yippy skippy," Zenoni muttered, faintly thinking of all the hours of his life sure to be dedicated to the painstaking task of untangling Christmas lights.

"At least I don't have you outside," Lorraine declared. "Tomorrow when you're working, I'm going to be up on the roof setting the elves around the sled. I had to push my book deadline ahead from January twenty-fourth to February ninth because of all this."

"My heart weeps for you," Zenoni replied sarcastically.

"Ha-ha," Lorraine retorted and rolled her eyes.

"I am happy you took the time to get some of the stuff up on the front lawn," Zenoni admitted. As soon as he pulled onto his street he had been greeted by eight-foot-high inflatable images of Frosty in a snow globe and a large moving Ferris wheel occupied by smiling elves.

"I figured someone had to do it," Lorraine replied, yet her

tone was docile and Zenoni heard no undertone of annoyance to the words.

For over an hour they worked tirelessly, changing bulbs and adjusting the miniature village collection. Zenoni had just started to untangle the strings of tree lights that had morphed into a messy ball when the telephone rang. Lorraine answered it with a happy "Hello," but her smile quickly dropped into a mask of horror as the voice on the other end of the line spoke.

"Oh my God, are you serious?" Lorraine cried into the speaker. "When was this? Was anyone hurt? I have no idea what's wrong with him either. Where is he now? Are they pressing charges?"

"What happened?" Zenoni asked.

Lorraine covered the mouthpiece with her hand. "It's Denise. Vincent's been arrested for property damage. He was caught deflating Christmas decorations on people's front lawns."

Zenoni simply shook his head, showing his wife that he was deeply disappointed in his nephew although, truth be told, he was far from flabbergasted. *I'm surprised he wasn't put in the slammer long before this,* Zenoni thought, turning his attention back to the tangled lights, thankful that his lawn ornaments had not experienced Vincent's destructive wrath.

"Okay, calm down," Lorraine was crooning into the phone. "No, of course I won't tell them about this! I promise. I'll be there within an hour. I'm coming right now. Try to stay calm, all right? I'll see you soon."

Lorraine set the phone into its cradle and looked solemnly at her husband. "You need to bail Vincent out," she announced.

"WHAT?" Zenoni roared, forsaking the lights.

"He's being held on five-hundred-dollar bail at the Castle Cove police station. Denise doesn't have the money to get him."

"Neither do we!" Zenoni exclaimed, feeling his face flush

with anger. "Do you think I can just reach into the tree and pull out wads of money? Where did you get the idea that we can afford to pay your nephew's bail?"

"At least we have savings. Denise struggles with everything now, you know that. Angelo, please—I know it's a lot to ask, but Denise is panicking; Vincent is all she has and she's terrified to lose him."

"How do you know he's not just going to go out and get in trouble again next week?" Zenoni demanded. "How is it that you're so sure this isn't just the beginning of a long string of arrests? To be honest, I'm surprised this is his first time behind bars; he's had serious problems for years! Now he's over eighteen, so this is going on his permanent record. You do realize that, don't you?"

"This is a hard time of year for them. Frank died right before Christmas and that always causes painful memories."

"Frank died after driving drunk. It's a miracle he didn't kill someone else in the process."

For this statement Lorraine had no answer.

"I don't want to be the bad guy here, Lorraine, but I also don't want to run around bailing Vincent out of jail every time he gets in trouble."

"I know that and I understand. I feel the same way. But he's also my nephew, our only nephew, and I don't want him in any more trouble. Angelo, please—it's Christmas, and Denise and I are afraid that Mom and Dad will find out about this. You know their health isn't great. I know it's a lot to ask, but he might listen to you if you get him out of trouble just this once. He misses his dad, he has no male role models, he—"

"He's nineteen, Lorraine, nineteen! That's above and beyond the age to know right from wrong. What is a nineteen-year-old doing deflating lawn ornaments? Was he drunk? Was he high? Do you even know?"

Lorraine said nothing, but kept her pleading eyes fixed on her husband.

"I really don't believe this," Zenoni snapped. "With everything I deal with all day and now this. It's never ending and I'm sick and tired of it. I'm not my nephew's keeper despite how I'm being treated! Can you imagine if the news got ahold of this one: the nephew of a detective working a front-page homicide case in jail? They'd have a field day. I'm sure my superiors would just love that one!" Yet even as he ranted, he grabbed his car keys and followed his wife out the door.

Denise lived a half hour away, and the drive to her modest garden apartment was tense. Zenoni sat behind the wheel staring straight ahead at the road as Lorraine, seated on the passenger side, stared out the side window at passing scenery.

Zenoni wasn't used to driving his civilian vehicle, a midsized Japanese-manufactured SUV, and he was trying not to drive too quickly. Nevertheless, his highway speed was increasing steadily, as if wishing to match the racing thoughts circling around his head.

Vincent needed a good smack upside his head; Zenoni had thought that for years. He was unruly, rude, and destructive. He lied like a snake oil salesman and, ever since he was young, he had been determined to have things his own way, no matter what the cost was to other people. Unfortunately, Vincent's idea of getting his own way and having fun usually consisted of wreaking some sort of destructive havoc. His life was a ceaseless quest to avoid boredom and Denise was usually on the short end of her son's careless deeds. She was the one who had to talk to angry teachers, deal with ranting neighborhood parents after Vincent somehow terrorized their children, and now she had to call her sister with the news that Vincent was in prison.

That poor woman has never had it easy with that kid, Zenoni's thoughts continued, as he clenched the steering

wheel in his palm. He remembered when Vincent was a tod-
dler; even back then he had an aversion to standing still and a
penchant toward temper tantrums. Of course his father had
done nothing but encourage his son's wild streak. Once,
Zenoni caught Frank—then well into his forties—standing in
the backyard teaching his then eight-year-old son to set off fire-
works. Likewise, Vincent had been introduced to the horse
track at a young age—his father's favorite place to be. In
Frank's mind, his only child could do no wrong. Vincent wor-
shipped his father, and after his death Vincent had become an
out-of-control hoodlum whom no one could quell. He had
been a lackluster student who terrified his teachers and peers
alike. Zenoni reckoned the school had thrown a party on the
day Vincent dropped out. His only comrades were other
street-dwelling troublemakers who knew no rules and set no
boundaries. Zenoni had always suspected that Vincent would
eventually end up on the wrong side of the law, but getting arrested for something like deflating lawn decorations was su-
perbly stupid, even for him.

While Zenoni was well aware of Vincent's capacity for
trouble, Lorraine was blind to it. She and Zenoni had been unable to have children, and she had soothed her inner pain and
aching disappointment by doting on her nephew. Vincent had
quickly caught on to his aunt's vulnerability and used it every
opportunity he got—at age seven he had even managed to con-
nive Lorraine into buying him four hundred dollars' worth of
Lego sets. On a few occasions, Zenoni attempted to tell Lorraine that Vincent was a manipulative little monster, but those
discussions usually ended with her in tears. Vincent was, she
claimed, the closest thing she would ever have to a child of her
own. Unable to argue with that fact, Zenoni eventually stopped
trying to enlighten his wife about their nephew's ill manners.
Yet this—bailing him out of prison—was something entirely

different. This was truly the last straw. Zenoni did not intend to ever rescue his wayward nephew from behind bars again, and the second he was left alone with the little thug, he planned to have a man-to-man talk with him—one in which neither his mother nor his aunt would be around to defend him.

Zenoni turned off the highway and drove through residential streets until he came to Denise's sand-colored home, which sat upon a shabby lawn. Vincent's sporty blue car was parked in the driveway. This surprised Zenoni greatly; usually Vincent and his car were inseparable. Denise was sitting on the front steps of her house waiting for her sister to arrive. She was wearing an old pair of jeans and an oversized burgundy sweatshirt. Her hair was tied back in a messy ponytail and she had no makeup on. From fifteen feet away, Zenoni could see that she looked strained and stressed to the point of being unhealthy.

No wonder Lorraine's worried about her, he thought, as he welled up with pity for his long-suffering sister-in-law, a sweet woman whose one fatal flaw was having been attracted to the wrong man.

"I'm sorry to have bothered you, but I didn't know what else to do," Denise sobbed as she ran toward the car. "I got a call from the police, and five hundred dollars is so much. I just didn't know what to do! Oh God, at times like this I miss Frank more than ever!"

Lorraine was out of the car and embracing her weeping sister before Zenoni was fully on the brake. "Don't worry. It's no problem," Lorraine exclaimed reassuringly. "You can always call us." Watching them together, Zenoni was struck by how much they resembled one another. If Denise was a few inches taller and a lot less stressed, she could have been Lorraine's double.

"You're such a sweet man, Angelo," Denise declared, peering

into the SUV. "I don't know what I can do to repay you for this—even a year's worth of meals wouldn't be nearly enough!"

"That's all right," Angelo quickly replied, horrified by the idea of suffering through another meal prepared by Denise. "You don't owe me a thing! We're family; don't even think of cooking me another meal! Please—you've really done more than enough."

Although his tone was pleasant and Denise seemed touched by the answer, Lorraine shot her husband a sharp this-is-no-time-to-be-a-food-critic glance.

"I'm so scared," Denise wailed. "Who knows what kind of weirdos they have him sharing a cell with!" As she spoke, she opened the back door and proceeded to climb into the SUV. "I can't believe my baby's in jail. I'm not even angry. I just want to see him home and safe before I figure out where I went wrong."

"Denise, it might be better if I go to the station alone," Zenoni suggested.

"But he's my son!" Denise cried, hovering halfway in and halfway out of the car.

"I know that, and I'll bring him home to you immediately. I just think it's better if I retrieve him solo. I'm an officer. I might be able to get some of his charges reduced."

This was an outright lie, but Zenoni was willing to say anything to prevent Denise from accompanying him to the station. She was in hysterics and capable of causing a scene if she were to tag along. Zenoni did not want his sister-in-law cited for outlandish behavior. Luckily, his lying words of comfort seemed to ease Denise somewhat.

"Are you serious?" she asked, looking at him the exact same way Lorraine did when she needed reassurance. "Can you really make them go easy on him?"

"I'll try, but I'm telling you that it will be more effective if I'm alone to talk with them, officer to officer."

"Come on," Lorraine added, tugging her sister's arm. "Angelo will get Vincent and bring him back safe and sound. In the meantime you and me can go have a cup of tea and you can tell me this whole story from start to finish."

Thankfully, Denise allowed herself to be led into the house and Zenoni headed off to the police station. It was a ten-minute drive from Denise's house, and Zenoni spent every second of it thinking about all the things he was going to say to his nephew. Oh yes—he would make sure this was one speech the rebellious little hooligan would never forget.

The Castle Cove police station was situated on the outskirts of a public park. Trees grew around the square concrete structure, giving it a more welcoming and scenic look than Zenoni's headquarters, but the inside was more or less identical. The cleaning fluid was the same and the familiar aroma of police work that filled Zenoni's nostrils quickly put him in the mood to interrogate his wayward nephew.

The booking sergeant at the front desk looked barely old enough to shave. His nametag identified him as Sergeant Neville. Zenoni explained his reason for being there, and Neville nodded and handed him paperwork to fill out. Ten minutes later, Zenoni surrendered five hundred dollars and was led to a bleak holding cell. Vincent was sitting alone inside it, looking comfortable and relaxed. He wasn't high or drunk, but neither was he concerned about being under arrest.

"You're free to go," Neville declared as he unlocked the door. Vincent coldly surveyed the sergeant and then shifted his eyes to his uncle. He tried to act indifferent, but Zenoni knew Vincent was startled; he had been expecting his mother.

Vincent regarded Zenoni with a nod, stood, hitched up his ridiculously large blue jeans, and casually exited his cell. Undaunted, he collected his wallet, cell phone, and shoes, which had been confiscated upon his arrival.

Wordlessly, Zenoni walked out of the police station toward the parking lot, with Vincent following closely behind him. As soon as they were inside Zenoni's forest green SUV, Vincent slouched down in the passenger seat, reached into his pants pocket, unwrapped a packet of gum, and popped it into his mouth.

"Where's my mom?" he asked casually.

"She's at home with Aunt Lorraine," Zenoni replied through clenched teeth. "She's a nervous wreck. Do you have any idea how stressful it is to get a phone call saying a loved one is in jail?"

Vincent shrugged. "How should I know? Nobody's ever given me a call like that."

"You are something else, do you know that?" Zenoni snapped. "You have just been arrested. Don't you understand? This is going on your permanent record! Is this getting through that thick skull of yours? This is serious, Vincent. This time you've really done it!"

"Can you just call me Vince? I hate being called Vincent."

"I am not interested in your personal likes and dislikes!" Zenoni roared, erupting into real rage. "If it was up to me you would have been in a military reform school years ago! Maybe that would have kept you out of jail! What is wrong with you? Did you fall down and hit your head or something, because I think it's gone all soft! Your mind doesn't seem to work right, that's for sure. What do you think you're doing by going onto people's lawns and deflating Christmas decorations?"

"We were bored," Vincent whined. "I was just having some

fun. The old bag who called the police overreacts to everything."

"Those ornaments are worth hundreds of dollars, Vincent—hundreds!" Zenoni shouted, recalling how a considerable portion of his annual income was spent on such items. "And you were trespassing on her property. I don't think she overreacted at all. You should count yourself lucky that she hasn't decided to sue you! Is that what you want, for your mother to lose the house because of the way you act? And what do you mean by 'we'? Were some of your hopeless little friends out there with you?"

Begrudgingly Vincent nodded. "It figures I'd be the only one to get pinched," he lamented. "My luck sucks."

"You created your own problems by hanging around with those punks, Vince," Zenoni spat sarcastically. "You don't go to school; you work at that mechanic shop surrounded by losers; you show no regard for your own mother—let alone your other family members. Is it really any wonder you get into trouble? Do you think we don't know about the drag-racing and the underage drinking and all the other bad things you get into? Do you think we're stupid? How do you think your mother feels about these little misadventures? You have to start thinking about her health, Vince. You're nineteen. That's not a baby. You're the man of the house now. When are you going to start acting like it?"

Vincent simply stared out the windshield saying nothing. He was a good-looking kid—tall with dark hair and darker eyes—yet he was unable to attract anything but a seemingly endless succession of sleepy-eyed girls devoid of depth or goals. According to Lorraine, Denise's biggest fear was being told that Vincent had gotten one—or more—of them pregnant. Thankfully, that was one indecency that had not come to pass . . . yet.

"Listen to me, Vince," Zenoni continued, as he reached out and gripped his nephew's shoulder. "Your mother can't take much more of this nonsense, and me and your Aunt Lorraine are sick of it as well. You have no idea how much pressure you put us all under, and you're digging your own grave in the process. You now have an arrest record. Do you realize how much harder that will make getting a job?"

Vincent simply stared silently at his uncle. Realizing that he was in no mood to talk, Zenoni cut right to the chase. "Your grandparents are coming up from Florida in a few weeks. They have no idea how much of a handful you are, and for the sake of their health and sanity, we are going to try to keep it that way. So, I am going to ask you to stay out of trouble until after the holidays. At least give us a nice Christmas, will you? Now, I don't care what happens at your court date. My guess is you'll get community service, but no matter what, I don't want you to let a word of this out to your grandparents. Keep your problems and your sharp mouth and your sneaky gazes to yourself. When they are up here, let's try to act like a normal family, if not for me then for your mother. *Capiche?*"

Vincent curtly nodded.

"Good. A small mercy from you after all this time," Zenoni replied and started up the engine. He was expecting a silent ride home and was surprised when Vincent broke the lull.

"Was my mom really upset? Like to the point that she wasn't doing too good?" He sounded distressed, despite the fact that he was trying hard to mask his emotions.

"Yes. You've got her worried sick. Your own mother! Does that make you happy, because sometimes I think you really enjoy getting into trouble."

"It wasn't my idea to wreck the stuff; it was my friend's plan."

"Well, you're just as bad for hanging around with those idiots. You have no one but yourself to blame for this, Vince."

"But you think if I stay out of trouble through Christmas—like to make sure Grandma and Grandpa don't worry—she'll feel better?" Incredibly, Vincent sounded honestly worried. It had been a long time since Zenoni had heard his nephew sound like he cared about anything.

"She'll be best off if you don't ever get in trouble again. I don't understand you—the first time you show any kind of concern at all about your actions is after you've established a police record. Nice going, kid. Just make sure to give us a trouble-free Christmas, okay? Your grandparents are older and they don't need this. None of us do."

Zenoni glanced briefly at Vincent, who met his eyes and nodded before turning away and staring out the window again. For the first time Zenoni felt as if his nephew had actually taken his advice to heart.

The remainder of the drive home was spent in silence. Vincent grew noticeably tenser as they approached his house. Zenoni had just pulled into the driveway when Denise ran out of the house melodramatically screaming for her son. Lorraine was running after her sister looking absolutely exhausted.

"Thank God you're all right!" Denise shrieked as she opened the door of the SUV and pulled Vincent out. "I was so sure you'd been hurt!" She was sobbing and holding onto her son as if he was an infant, despite the fact that he was over a foot taller than her and nearly twice her weight. After embracing him for the better half of a minute Denise released her son, grabbed him by the shoulders, and shook him. "What is wrong with you?" she demanded to know, weeping. "Why would you do something this stupid, Vincent? You'll carry this for the rest of your life, and you did it right before Christmas too! Are you trying to destroy yourself? Because you're succeeding and taking me with you!"

"He's agreed to behave himself so your parents won't know of this," Zenoni interrupted. Denise looked at him suspiciously.

"Are you serious?" she asked her son.

Vincent nodded. He was staring at the ground, unable to make eye contact with his mother.

"Get in the house!" Denise ordered before turning to Zenoni. "Thank you again for everything."

"I do what I can," Zenoni replied. "Take care of yourself."

Denise nodded and started to walk to her house, when she turned back toward Zenoni and added, bizarrely, "Good luck with the decorating."

"Thanks," Zenoni answered, amazed that Christmas ornaments were not to be forgotten even in the midst of a family crisis. He remained seated in the car as he waited for Lorraine, who was giving her sister a good-bye hug. Denise looked more dismayed than ever. It really was amazing she had clung to her sanity for so long. Sometimes when he saw the stress Vincent put his mother through, Zenoni was glad he and Lorraine had no children. Yet that was a deeply secret thought, one of the very few he would never share with his wife.

As Zenoni looked out at the embracing sisters, he said a silent prayer that Vincent would allow for a peaceful holiday season. Denise certainly deserved one.

Chapter Fifteen

Arnold Genson was not happy about being called into the police station at nine o'clock on a Saturday morning. Saturday was a busy day for the jewelry television studio and he felt that he was losing valuable time by being with the police. His displeasure was immediately obvious to anyone who looked upon his grim face as he sat in Interview Room One tapping his pudgy fingers on the desk. He glared angrily at Zenoni the moment the detective entered the room.

"Good morning, Mr. Genson," Zenoni chirped, making extra sure his sarcasm was blatant.

"It's not for me," Arnold snapped.

"You sound a bit testy. Was the fishing no good?"

"For your information I did snag two fluke, but both were too small to keep. Mostly I went to relax after all the stress you've put me through. Why am I here? I've already told you everything I know."

"We got some information from a source who claims to have witnessed Tiffany arguing with you, heatedly, over the phone."

"What source would this be?"

"That doesn't matter. What does matter is that we're taking this very seriously."

Zenoni sat and started to record the interview as Arnold glared at his watch.

"I should be at work now."

"The sooner you tell us the truth, the sooner we can resolve this."

"I *have* told you the truth," Arnold declared through clenched teeth. "It's not my problem that you chose not to believe it. I came right out and told you that she was hard to deal with and often shouted at me both in person and over the phone."

Zenoni took a moment to study Arnold's face. His expression was one of severe annoyance and his tone was becoming increasingly hostile. *This is what Vincent's gonna be like in a few years,* Zenoni thought, feeling anger surge inside of him. He had not slept well and he was in no mood for coy games.

"We have information that suggests you were involved in a heated dispute with Tiffany Kehl at the end of October. A witness overheard her informing you that she had information about you that could prove detrimental to your career. Our witness tells us that she was threatening to use this information against you if you tried to oust her from her job. Do you remember that conversation?"

"I wish I knew who this source is. I—"

"Answer the question, Mr. Genson," Zenoni ordered, sounding as tough as Wildow usually was in the interrogation room. Arnold was growing visibly uneasy. He was sweating profusely and, like Vincent, he was having difficulty making eye contact, opting to stare at the tabletop instead of his interviewer.

"Yes," Arnold unwillingly answered.

"So—what was this dirt she had on you?"

No reply from Arnold.

"You're only making this harder on yourself, Mr. Genson. We can sit here all day if you like."

Arnold shot Zenoni a long, hard look. "If I tell you, do you promise I can get out of here?"

"The sooner you talk, the sooner we can leave the room, yes."

Arnold took a few moments to collect his thoughts and then began to speak slowly and carefully; his eyes remained locked on the surface of the desk. He sounded as if every word he spoke caused him physical pain. "Tiffany was a problem. She had a bad attitude and she would do anything to get her way. I'm going to be completely honest: I hate my job. I mean, I despise it, loath it, detest it—absolute hatred. It's demanding, it's unending, and it's completely overwhelming. I'm not an organized person and files *do* get misplaced from time to time. She knew I was struggling and she never tried to help once— oh no, not Tiffany. She just picked and picked at everything I did, which only added to my stress. Look, I'm starting to get an ulcer and sometimes I need a break. So, I came to work late, I took extended lunches, and I left a little earlier than I should have. No one else cared, but she knew everything. Usually she said she liked it better when I wasn't around, but then something would get lost and it was all my fault. I'm telling you, the woman was a nightmare! After a while I couldn't take it anymore. I honestly thought she was going to drive me crazy. I was trying to have her transferred to another studio upstate—needless to say, she wasn't very impressed when she found out about my plan. She started to threaten me. She told me that if I dared to have her transferred she would have the CEOs investigate me. She said she had enough documented proof of my continuing absences to have me fired. I was being blackmailed!"

"It also sounds like you were being negligent in your work," Zenoni replied unsympathetically.

"I was overly stressed."

"Aren't we all? How did you react to her threats?"

"Well, I got angry, of course. I shouted at her and she shouted back at me. That is the fundamental makeup of an argument, you know," Arnold sneered.

"Is it the fundamental makeup of murder?" Zenoni retorted.

"What is wrong with you people?" Arnold demanded, his face flushed with rage as he banged his fists on the table hard enough to shake the walls of the room. "You know I'm innocent; you already checked my alibi!"

"True," Zenoni replied coolly, "but Tiffany was killed between two and three in the morning. You left the bowling alley at around two and then, according to your version of events, went right home. However, technically speaking, we have no concrete evidence that proves you went straight to your house. So, you still could have done it had you stopped into the studio before going home."

"You have no evidence against me at all," Arnold hissed. "Everything you say is just speculation. You have nothing substantial; you're grasping at straws. I'll tell you, if I was in your shoes, I would stop questioning me and start asking the security guard about his role in all of this."

"Which guard?" Zenoni asked, grateful that Arnold had finally supplied a lead.

"Konrad Stewart. About two weeks ago I was walking out of the building and heard Tiffany screaming at him about what an 'incompetent fool' he was—those were her exact words. Mind you, it was far from surprising to hear her yell at people but, incredibly, Konrad was actually talking back to her. He kept telling her to get off his back, because the problems weren't all his fault. He actually had the nerve to tell her that she had to start treating people with more respect before her mouth 'got her killed'—that's exactly how he phrased it. I wanted to congratulate him—he's a far braver man than I am to have spoken to her in such a way—but the argument sounded like it was turning ugly, and I just wanted to get home and away from my job as soon as possible."

"It's a compelling story, Mr. Genson. Why didn't you tell us all of this the first time you were interviewed?"

"I didn't think it was of any importance. Tiffany fought with everyone at one time or another. But, since you insist on wasting more of my time, I assume that I should tell you every little detail so that I am not inconvenienced further. I have no idea if her argument with the guard had anything at all to do with her death; you'd really have to ask him. He doesn't work on weekends, so he might be home as we speak. I just mention this since he did say her mouth could get her killed one day and then—boom—less than a month later she's dead. At the time I thought he was just letting off steam, but since you are determined to overanalyze everything, I might as well too."

"Okay, now is there anything else you'd like to share with us?" Zenoni persisted. "Any little detail at all? Realize that if you fail to mention something that concerns you when we find out about it—and I assure you we *will* find out—we're going to have to talk to you again. Obviously you don't like being disturbed, so if you have anything else to say, I think it would be wise to say it now."

"Really, I've racked my brain and I can honestly say that I didn't see or hear anything else even slightly suspicious."

"Then I thank you for your time, Mr. Genson. I'll make sure to contact you if I need anything else."

"I sincerely hope you don't," Arnold spat as he rose from his seat. "I've already been disrupted too many times because of this—you know I didn't do it and I do not appreciate being spoken to like a suspect!"

And I do not appreciate being spoken to rudely by a pest, Zenoni thought, biting his tongue to keep from blurting out the words. Because of his trying evening the night before, he had been forced to swallow his sarcasm all morning long.

Ten minutes later Arnold was away from the premises of the police station and Zenoni was taking a breather in the station break room. He gulped down a cup of freshly brewed coffee, grimaced with the sharp pain from his outraged stomach lining, and gazed out the office window at the street below. As he watched cars pass by he wondered what the drivers' lives were like; at that moment he wished he could change places with another person just to see if that would make things any easier.

"Is everything okay?" Wildow asked, joining his partner in crime-stopping. He had worked with Zenoni long enough to know that when he got this quiet, something was wrong.

"Not really," Zenoni replied, turning away from the window and chuckling in pure frustration. "Vincent got arrested last night."

"You're kidding," Wildow replied. His eyes were wide with alarm.

"Unfortunately I'm not. The little punk has been getting in trouble since he was old enough to walk; yet he only gets arrested after he's eighteen so it goes on his permanent record. How's that for idiotic?"

"What did he do?"

"That's the worst part—he got arrested for property damage, wrecking Christmas ornaments on people's front lawns! What kind of a numbskull does that—let alone at age nineteen! He was cold sober too! I'm telling you, there's something wrong with that kid."

"How's Lorraine taking it?"

"She and her sister are nervous wrecks. I thought Denise—Vincent's mother—was going to have a nervous breakdown. I had to go to the local police station to pick him up, five hundred dollars in bail, and he didn't even seem upset about being arrested! For all I know, this is some kind of rite of passage among the little creeps he hangs around with."

"What are you going to do about him?"

"I don't know. I really haven't a clue. I told him he'll probably get community service and I'll personally see to it that he follows that commitment. Right now we're just trying to get through Christmas. His grandparents are coming up from Florida and all we want is for him to behave himself and spare them the truth of his newly established rap sheet. It's just a load of unnecessary stress to deal with."

"I'll say," Wildow replied. "At least he didn't hurt anyone."

Zenoni nodded. The only good thing that could be said of Vincent's illegal endeavor was that no one had been seriously injured or killed. That made him considerably less guilty than whoever had murdered Tiffany Kehl.

"Anyway," Zenoni declared, setting his empty coffee mug on the counter, "what do you think we should do about this Konrad guy?"

"He was the one with the sealed juvenile record, right?"

Zenoni nodded. "He also doesn't have a solid alibi. He said he was at home at the time of the murder, but we have no concrete evidence to back up his claim."

"Well, I think we better go talk to him then. He's off weekends, so maybe if we take a drive to his place and surprise him at home, we'll catch him off guard and get more information out of him."

"Agreed," Zenoni replied. "Mind you, he's under no obligation to speak to us, but if he's really as innocent as he claims, then he'll have no reason to mind sparing us a few moments to discuss the case."

The detectives took a couple of minutes to look up Konrad on the computer. A quick search of the license database informed them of his address.

"If he's not home when we get there, we'll park nearby and wait," Zenoni declared as he zipped up his coat and fished through his pockets until his palm closed around his car keys. "If we can get this case solved before the week is through, my Christmas wish will have come true."

Chapter Sixteen

Konrad Stewart lived in a lower-middle-class suburban neighborhood known as Deer River. His home was a 1950s-era split-level yellow ranch that was showing signs of serious weathering. Yet it was not the poorly kept lawn or the drawn curtains that made the detectives wary of the house. It was the ten-foot-tall steel mesh fence that encircled it and the half dozen snarling Rottweilers behind it.

"Are you sure this is the right place?" Wildow asked, praying that he had been taken to the wrong location.

Zenoni checked his notes. "This is the address listed."

"I was afraid you were going to say that."

"Why would a security guard at a mediocre jewelry television studio need guard dogs protecting his house?" Zenoni asked, noting that the residence was a far cry from a high-class dwelling that would normally require such intense security.

"Maybe he's in the Witness Protection Program," Wildow suggested, grinning. He often confronted unusual circumstances with humor.

"At this point nothing surprises me," Zenoni replied, killing the engine and swinging the car door open.

"How are we going to get to the front door?" Wildow asked as he and Zenoni walked toward the massive gate. "I don't see any way to get to the doorbell."

Zenoni was pondering the same dilemma when the dogs

started to bark and snarl frantically. The closer the detectives got to the gate, the more aggressive the animals became. The larger ones were throwing their bodies against the fence, saliva flowing freely from their upturned jaws. The hysteria of the Rottweilers served as a guest announcement to Konrad, who soon appeared in the doorway of his home shouting commands for the canines to be silent. He scurried down his front porch steps reassuring the dogs with firm pats on the head. As soon as the animals laid eyes upon their husky master, they replaced their heavy barking with docile silence.

"Detectives? What are you doing here?" Konrad asked. He seemed surprised by their presence, but not the least bit hostile as he unlocked the gate and ushered them onto his property with a wide smile. Neither detective was thrilled about stepping into the dogs' territory, but the creatures were calm in the presence of Konrad, so Zenoni had faith that he would not be ripped to shreds before he reached the house.

"Never mind the dogs. They like to tell me every time somebody's at the door," Konrad explained. "I'm sorry I didn't come sooner. I was out back trying to clean the leaves out of my rain gutters. Leaves are the worst part of fall, I think. This chore should have been done two weeks ago, but I kept putting it off."

Zenoni took note of Konrad's muddy and soggy work jeans and sweatshirt. Cleaning out the gutters was a chore he himself vehemently detested.

"What's with the dogs?" Wildow asked suddenly, looking uneasily from one animal to the next.

"Oh, don't mind them," Konrad declared, chuckling at the look of trepidation on Wildow's face. "They look tough, but they're nothing but a bunch of puppy dogs."

"Sure, I bet. Why do you have so many?"

"I rescue, train, and occasionally breed them," Konrad replied as he opened his front door and welcomed the detectives into his home. "They're a great breed—very loyal and smart. You can teach them to scare the bejesus out of trespassers but still be big teddy bears to their master."

By now the men were standing in Konrad's living room. It was a tiny space, made smaller by clutter—secondhand furniture and dozens of dog toys—yet it was undeniably cozy. In Zenoni's opinion, the only truly unpleasant thing about the room was the odor of the dogs, which had not been removed from the area despite heavy use of air sanitizers.

"It must be a hassle raising all those dogs," Wildow commented, as he eyeballed his surroundings.

"It sure is, but I love the work," Konrad replied. "It's expensive, though. I actually work with a Rottweiler rescue agency that helps pick up the tab. Can I get you guys anything? Coffee maybe?"

"No thanks," Wildow said, quickly rebuffing the offer.

"Same here," Zenoni added. His stomach lurched at the mere thought of any more caffeine. It was time to get down to business. "Mr. Stewart, we have information that claims you were seen arguing with Tiffany Kehl shortly before her death. Do you have any recollection of that incident?"

Konrad reclined in his chair and nodded. "Do you mean a few weeks ago? Well, yeah, like I said in my first statement, we argued every now and then—rather, she yelled at me about stuff that was out of my control."

"According to this report, the argument got pretty heated and you apparently did some yelling back at her."

"It was a bad day for me."

"Do you care to explain that?"

"It's like I said—I had a rough day. One of my first dogs, as in one of the first ones I ever rescued from a city junkyard, died the day before. She had a good life and died of old age— she wasn't harmed or nothing—but that didn't stop me from hurting. So I come into work the next day and Tiffany starts yelling at me about the cameras being down. She was also having trouble finding a tray of gems that was supposed to have been delivered the previous night, and for some reason she assumed that was my fault too. I didn't even work the previous day, so between the death of Tuffy—that was my dog—and her screeching, I just lost my cool and started yelling. I told her she needed to start treating people a little better. She could be really sharp-tongued."

"We were told you let her know that you thought her sharp mouth could result in her death," Wildow replied. "Did you mean that as a threat? Because, I've got to tell you, it's pretty suspicious that you were heard saying those words less than a month before the woman was found dead."

"Now wait just a minute," Konrad exclaimed, leaning forward in his seat. "I did say that to her, but I didn't mean it as a threat! I had no idea this was going to happen and I never would have wished it on her or anybody. When I said that, I was just letting off steam, and I thought I was doing her a favor. She seriously could have worked on her people skills."

"But the argument didn't escalate past yelling?" Zenoni questioned.

"Of course not! Listen, I don't yell often. I learned to control my temper when I was young; but when I do get mad, it's for a reason. That day she provoked me. All I did was answer her back—nothing less and certainly nothing more."

"Did you ever get angry with her prior to that?"

"Sure, but that was the only time I ever actually talked back to her. She was the kind of person who liked to pick fights, and once you engaged her, she refused to get off your back. I think part of her really enjoyed combat with words." Konrad looked from one detective's face to the other, leaned back, and sighed. "I'm going to be really honest with you because I have a feeling you already know about my juvenile record. You're both looking at me like I'm a ticking time bomb. I didn't get that record for doing something violent. I got that record for trying to steal a television. When I was growing up, it was rough, and we didn't have a lot of money, and one Christmas when I was fifteen, I tried—and failed—to steal a TV from this electronics store by my house. My options were to either go to juvenile hall or take an anger management class with community service since I fought with the arresting officers. Anyway, I took the latter option, and it was the best thing that ever happened to me. That class helped me control my temper for life. It takes a lot to set me off now. Tiffany was annoying and she could be downright verbally abusive, but I would never have hurt her or anyone else."

Zenoni nodded, happy to finally know what Konrad's juvenile record was for.

"And, in case you're wondering how I got into dogs," Konrad continued, while staring at Nolan Wildow, who was nervously peering out the window at the Rottweilers in the front yard, "my community service was at an animal shelter. At first I was slow to go, but I grew to love that work to the point of being obsessive. I volunteered there even after my sentence was up and I got really into Rottweilers. This one cop who was on the K-9 unit heard about me and hooked me up with the rescue agency. His name was Nathan; he was a really nice guy. He trained dogs for the police, German shepherds mostly, and he taught me German commands to train my dogs with. He said it was safer if you train them in another language, more effective. That's the work I love, training the dogs; I just stick with security jobs to make some extra cash. I'm a big guy and I haven't had much trouble finding work in that field. Does that satisfy your curiosity?"

Both Zenoni and Wildow nodded. The guard had gone out

of his way to be helpful and, Zenoni had to admit, his words sounded genuine.

"And yes, I stick by my story," Konrad offered, before the question was even asked. "I have no hard-core proof that I was here, but I'm telling you I was home and asleep when Tiffany was killed. I have nothing to hide, even if I don't have a strong alibi."

Nothing's new with him, Zenoni thought, feeling more than a little disappointed. This visit, although fairly painless, had been for nothing. Zenoni rose in his seat and was about to thank Konrad when the larger man spoke again, this time in a contemplative—almost cautious—tone of voice.

"There is one other thing, but it's just a hunch. I have no proof or anything, but if I were you, I'd keep my eyes on Hector Harte, the janitor."

"And why is that?" Zenoni asked. He kept his voice even, but his adrenaline was up at the thought of a new lead.

Konrad shrugged. "I just got a strong feeling that he's got ten sticky fingers. It just seems to me that the cameras break down a lot, and more stuff goes missing, whenever he's around."

"Are you sure?"

"Yes. I got nothing concrete on the guy, but when he comes on shift, he's evasive and sneaky. I'm telling you, there's something weird with him. Stuff would just vanish and the cameras wouldn't catch it, because they either weren't working or had been turned off."

"How would Hector have access to the cameras?"

"I have no idea. He acts right enough whenever I'm around, but he usually works the night shift, so I'm off duty during most of his hours. He knows the place inside out, so he probably knows how mostly everything works. The janitors fix the cameras when they malfunction, so they obviously have some understanding of how they work. Again, I'm not really sure if this has any merit at all, or if I should even be saying it, but I want to be as helpful as I can. I really can't shake the feeling that Hector's connected to this somehow. The guy gives me the creeps."

"Is there anything else?"

"No, man. I just hope I did you some good on the case. After everything that's gone down this past week, I'm really sorry I yelled at Tiffany the way I did. For all her faults, she wasn't a bad person."

The detectives thanked Konrad for his time and vacated the premises. Wildow's chest was tight with fear as he walked through the dog-filled yard, but not one of the Rottweilers as much as snarled at him. They seemed as harmless and docile as stuffed toys . . . big stuffed toys.

"What do you think?" Wildow asked, as he lowered himself into the passenger seat of the car. "Should we pay Hector a visit?"

"I don't see why not," Zenoni said, as he leafed through his notebook. "It's our only lead and Konrad seems to be on the level. According to my notes, Hector is off weekends too, so, with a little luck, he'll be home today. We have his address on record; it hasn't changed since that petty theft arrest back in the 1990s. Let's just see if we can get anything new out of him on a surprise visit. I've been meaning to question him again. Since the first time I met him I thought he was hiding something."

Zenoni started the engine and began the long drive to Hector Harte's residence in the town of Oakwood.

Chapter Seventeen

Oakwood was far out on the Island. It was a rural community that dangled somewhere between working class and dirt-poor on the economic ladder. The rundown stores and beat-up homes that occupied the area highlighted its humble demographics.

The detectives arrived at Hector's dilapidated mobile home a little after two o'clock in the afternoon. It sat among a number of other rusting trailers atop an unpaved dirt road. Zenoni parked carefully out front, making sure not to hit an aging red pickup situated beside his vehicle.

Thank God it's not supposed rain today, Zenoni thought, as he killed the engine and stepped out of the car. He could imagine how difficult it would be to maneuver his car away from this area if all the dirt beneath his feet turned into mud.

The detectives took a moment to survey their surroundings. Hector's was number 37 in a long line of rusting trailer homes. There were small patches of dying grass in front of most of the homes; Hector's lawn was dotted with numerous weather-worn ceramic ornaments. Across the way, two young children stared curiously at the detectives from atop their tricycles. Three houses down on Hector's side of the street, an old man in a camouflage-print cap sat in an ancient lawn chair. He stared at the two men in suits for perhaps ten seconds, then spit out the tobacco he had been chewing and turned away. Somewhere in the distance, a hound dog was barking.

"It's like something out of *My Name Is Earl*," Wildow remarked.

"I was thinking the same thing," Zenoni agreed, even though he had never watched an episode of *My Name Is Earl* in his life. "Let's just see what this guy has to say and then get out of here."

Although the curtains were drawn, Zenoni could clearly hear two squabbling voices coming from inside the trailer. He sighed as he made his way up to the door. He hated to walk into an argument, but at least someone was home.

The doorbell was broken, so Zenoni had to knock on the door—hard—to be heard over the shouting. A woman answered the door. She was of medium height, but made to look taller with her four-inch heels. Although obviously in her forties and somewhat overweight, she had squeezed herself into tight jeans and a low-cut top to look like a teenager. Zenoni had never seen someone with such long artificial nails, and he'd be willing to bet that there were clowns who wore less makeup.

"Who are you and what do you want?" she demanded, scowling at the officers distrustfully.

The lawmen held out their badges. "I'm Detective Zenoni, and this is my partner, Detective Wildow. We're here to speak with Hector. Is he around?"

"What's he done now?" the woman asked, her eyes fiery with rage.

"He's not charged with anything—we just want to have a few words with him."

"Do you hear that?" the woman screamed, turning her head to look over her shoulder. With the same quick movement, she opened the door fully, exposing a messy living room. The floor was covered in empty and discarded potato chip bags, the furniture was old and in desperate need of new upholstery, and the walls were bare except for a framed photo of Elvis above a dartboard. Hector Harte was sitting in a large reclining chair in front of an old television. On the screen, dozens of cars were zooming around a racetrack. He held a cigarette in his left hand and a can of beer in his right. The remote was sitting atop his considerable stomach. His only apparel was a pair of white socks and blue boxer shorts.

"Woman, I'm not telling you again—shut your mouth!" he shouted, never removing his eyes from the television. "The NASCAR highlights are on and this is my day off. Save your whining for your friends!"

"The police are here for you! And I don't care what you've done this time, I'm not spending another penny of my money to bail you out!"

"What the heck are you talking about?" Hector asked, as he turned his head and saw the officers. "What are you doing here?" he demanded. "I already told you all I know!"

"What's this about?" the woman asked the detectives. "He's always up to something, but you'll have to tell me what, because I can't even keep track of all the bad stuff he gets himself into."

"Can I get your name please, ma'am?" Zenoni queried carefully, ready to take notes.

"Margaret Bethany Scott," she declared briskly. "I'm this louse's wife as far as the common law goes. He's too lazy to even make it official."

"That's enough from you!" Hector exclaimed angrily and then turned toward the detectives. "Is this about the Kehl woman?"

Zenoni nodded. "Yup, I'm afraid it is."

"Murder?" Margaret cried. "Now you've got yourself in

trouble with murder? I knew you were bad news but I never thought you'd get mixed up in something like that!" Turning away from Hector, Margaret gazed nervously at the detectives. "I've been with him since 1985 and he's never been involved with something like this."

"He's not in trouble yet, ma'am," Wildow reassured her. "We just want to have a few words with him."

"Well, that's just fine with me!" Margaret spat, obviously trying to control her temper. "In fact, you can arrest him and haul his tobacco- and alcohol-soaked hide off to jail, and I won't care one little bit. I've already seen too much over too many years, and I was heading out anyway. Good luck, Hector. I'm going shopping."

"Good riddance!" Hector screamed, as Margaret grabbed the keys to the truck and stormed out of the trailer. Seconds later, the sound of tires screeching could be heard from outside.

Forget My Name Is Earl*; this is full blown* Jerry Springer, Zenoni thought as he turned back toward Hector, who was staring at him hatefully.

"Now look at what you done," he snarled. "My woman's left me again."

"My condolences," Wildow replied flippantly. "We've got a few questions for you about your activities at the workplace."

"I'm a janitor. I clean stuff. That's all," Hector sneered.

"We have information that suggests you are doing more than cleaning."

"What's that supposed to mean?"

"Mr. Harte, did you ever hear Tiffany say that gemstones went missing from the studio?"

"I reckon I did once or twice," Hector said, his eyes narrowing into hostile slits.

"Some people are saying that stuff goes missing twice as often whenever you're around."

"What people?"

"That's not important."

"I hope you don't mean that no-good head of security who can't learn to mind his own business!" Hector screeched, truly outraged. "He's got a record, you know, from when he was a kid. I heard him saying that to one of the part-timers one day, real conversational, like he wasn't even ashamed of it or nothing. You're two dang fools for listening to the ramblings of a junior ex-con."

"Let me remind you, Mr. Harte, that you also have a record and yours is an adult one."

"Aw, never mind that stupid old thing!" Hector declared, as he stubbed out his cigarette on the lid of an empty beer can. "I was twenty-two, broke, and a little drunk. I had a thirst for more so I went into a quickie mart, distracted the clerk by throwing down some magazines, and stole a six-pack. How was I supposed to know the store had security cameras? At least I wasn't drinking underage and I didn't hold nobody up with a weapon!"

"Well, that justifies everything," Wildow replied sarcastically.

"I never did jail time neither. Margaret came and bailed me out."

"Well, weren't you a lucky duck?" Wildow exclaimed before continuing his questioning in a serious tone. "Now, tell us, do you have any knowledge or know-how of why all these jewels disappeared? Because if you do I suggest you tell us now."

"And why's that?"

"Because I'm starting to think that you have something to do with the missing gems, and Tiffany found out about it, so you dealt with her. You know, fixed it so she wouldn't be able to tell anybody what she knew."

This suggestion startled Hector so much that he almost spit

out his beer. He gazed at the detectives goggle-eyed and waved his hands in an "I didn't do it" gesture until he was able to swallow his beverage and speak.

"Now, you know that's a lie!" he proclaimed. "I stole some beer. I could never kill nobody. Even that nagging sack of annoyance I live with told you that."

"So you're completely at a loss as to what happened to Tiffany—but what about the missing gems? I'm asking if you know anything about those."

"No! And I know you got nothing real bad on me or I'd be arrested by now. If you came just because of what that halfwit rent-a-cop said, then you've wasted your time. I didn't do a dang thing and I know nothing about what happened neither. Now will you get off my property and stop wasting my time? I don't have many days when I can sit around and enjoy my cable, you know."

It had been a long time since Zenoni felt as defeated as he did leaving Hector Harte's house. Instinctively, he knew the janitor was hiding something, but without proper basis for an arrest warrant there was no chance of interrogating him.

"We came all this way for nothing," Zenoni spat as he backed out of the dirt-road driveway. "He didn't give us anything to work with at all!"

"I still got a feeling he knows more than he's saying," Wildow replied.

"Ditto," Zenoni declared, lowering his foot onto the accelerator. *So much for solving this one anytime soon.*

Chapter Eighteen

As soon as Zenoni entered the police station, he marched straight to Sandra's desk and asked her to look up Margaret Bethany Scott in the police database.

"Who's she?" Sandra asked, typing the name. Zenoni noticed her nails were ready for Christmas—each one painted red with a little green Christmas tree in the center.

"She's a suspect's common-law wife and, considering the kind of rocky relationship she's in, some sort of domestic dispute history wouldn't surprise me in the least."

"Well, you can start being surprised now," Sandra declared matter-of-factly, staring at her computer screen. "Margaret Bethany Scott has absolutely no police record of any kind."

"Figures," Zenoni exclaimed, throwing his hands into the air out of pure frustration. "We've got nothing, totally zip. I'm taking an early night. I'll file today's report tomorrow. Sandra, please call me if anything regarding this case comes up."

"Will do."

Zenoni gave his secretary a nod of approval and walked into his private office. He had left his thermos on his desk and wanted to collect it so it could be cleaned that night. If there was one thing Lorraine was paranoid about, it was mold collecting on unwashed food containers. Zenoni was expecting to grab the thermos and leave immediately, but when he opened his office door, he got the surprise of his life.

Several animated singing Christmas ornaments in the form of toys and popular culture icons had been placed in various locations around his office. Elmo wearing a Santa hat chimed an evil squeaky version of "Jingle Bells," as he shook his mechanical hips and furiously waved two small bells in his furry red hands. All colors of the M&M mascots were crammed into a sleigh and jamming to their own rendition of "We Wish You a Merry Christmas." Snoopy and Woodstock, perched atop a smiling Christmas tree, instructed Zenoni to "Have a Holly-Jolly Christmas." Bugs Bunny and Daffy Duck dressed as Saint Nick grooved to the tune of "Jingle Bell Rock," as the Pillsbury Doughboy, equipped with a shiny red Rudolph-like nose, declared, "It's the Most Wonderful Time of the Year." There were over a half dozen other figurines, but Zenoni was too shocked to pay them any attention. This was the first time he had ever been assaulted by musical toys in the workplace. The various overlapping melodies playing all at once sounded like an orchestra from the underworld. Zenoni supposed it would have been funny if he wasn't so taken by surprise—and if it had been happening to someone other than himself.

"What in God's name—" he began when Sandra, Wildow, and a few college-age office interns burst into laughter behind him.

"Merry Christmas," Sandra giggled. "Do you like your gifts?"

"This was your doing?"

"Nolan helped."

Zenoni cocked an eye at his partner.

"It was Sandra's idea; she and the others set it all up. I just brought some if the props—call it an early Christmas gift."

"You're so thoughtful," Zenoni replied sarcastically, trying to disguise his amusement. "And you," he declared, turning to his secretary, "don't you have better things to do on a Saturday a few weeks before Christmas?"

Playfully Sandra shook her head. "Not at all. I'm working every day until the twenty-third of December, and then I've got until January eighth off. I'm taking my sister's two kids to Disney World. The kids don't even know they're going yet. The tickets will be their stocking-stuffer surprise."

"They'll love that," Zenoni replied, sincerely impressed by the gift.

"And your wife will love those decorations," Sandra replied, running her eyes all over the office. "We set this whole thing up knowing how much she loves getting you into the holiday spirit."

Zenoni laughed as he walked around the office, switching the figurines off and gathering them into a large plastic garbage bag.

"Hey! We paid good money for those," Sandra shouted, horrified by the sight of the trash bag.

"Don't worry. I'm not throwing them away. I'm just transporting them to my car. I have a feeling my wife will be very surprised."

"*You* certainly were," Sandra replied, smiling.

"Yes, I was, and you will be too when you get the hospital bill," Zenoni retorted. "I have an ulcer. If I'm driven to some sort of psychosis due to relentless off-key Christmas tunes, I'm holding you totally accountable. Stop smiling! I could have you for harassment!"

Sandra simply rolled her eyes and walked off, giving Zenoni a small good-bye wave as he zipped up his coat, grabbed his almost-forgotten thermos, and slung the decoration-filled trash bag over his shoulder. He felt like a homeless version of Saint Nicholas as he left the station. Cynically, he wondered if this incident would lead to future back problems. One thing was certain: this was the strangest gift he'd ever received, yet somehow one of his favorites.

* * *

Lorraine was definitely surprised to see her husband home so early, but she was even more amazed by the numerous singing ornaments—all equipped with working batteries—in his possession.

"This was your co-workers' doing?" Lorraine asked, laughing as she inspected a red-suited version of Darth Vader.

"Creative, huh?"

"I think they're great! I can't believe it, but I don't think we have any of these yet. We'll have to find a place for one in every room of the house."

"Your father will *love* that," Zenoni said. His father-in-law was even more easily peeved by tacky holiday memorabilia than he was.

"Well, this at least takes my mind off the Christmas card list. It gets bigger and bigger every year. I'm so glad we ordered the cards early."

Zenoni nodded, unhappy to be reminded that they had selected "Season's Greetings" cards before Halloween.

"So, you're home for the rest of the day?" Lorraine asked.

"Unless I get a call."

"Okay, what are your plans for today then?"

"Well, I'd like to relax in front of the television, but I assume I better get some of this decorating done. The boxes are starting to take over the house."

"Oh, good!" Lorraine cried. "I don't want to keep nagging you, but I really had no idea how else I was going to get all of this done. I hate to tell you, but I don't think I tied the lawn ornaments down right. I tried to reinforce them after I inflated them, but I've never done it before. It's always your job. So you better go check to make sure they're okay. The weather report says a storm's coming in tonight with strong winds, and I don't want those things taking flight."

"I'll deal with it in a minute," Zenoni replied, as he walked into his bedroom and changed out of his work clothes. He could already see the reaction of his next-door neighbor, Eoghan, if a giant ornament got loose and crashed into his house.

I'd be sued in a second, Zenoni thought. *Perhaps the courts would award him some of the dancing pop culture icons in damages.*

When Zenoni stepped outside he saw that Eoghan's wife, Kate, was out in her yard trimming the hedges. Her three-year-old son, Sean, was sitting at her feet, watching gleefully as his breath made clouds in the cold air. The little boy looked like the Michelin Man in his heavily padded white snowsuit. Zenoni gave them a smile and a wave as he inspected the ornaments, which did indeed need to be tied down tighter.

Good thing I came home early, Zenoni thought, wondering what Melody Zielinski and the rest of the press hounds would have to say if a lawn decoration of his got loose and destroyed the home of a neighbor so close to Christmas.

There was much more work to be done in Zenoni's home than he'd initially thought. He had gotten so far behind in the decorating that the holiday chore list seemed insurmountably long. After dotting the path leading to their front door with enormous plastic candy canes, he helped Lorraine string lights on the roof. Then it was onto placing cotton wool around the Christmas village to make it appear as if a blizzard had hit the tiny community. The last task of the evening was doing the final touches on the tree—the top of its pole had been standing branchless in the living room for days and Lorraine was sick of looking at it.

"Napoleon, get away from there!" Zenoni shouted, as he watched his eleven-year-old cat dive into the center of the cardboard box containing the artificial branches. "What's with you today?" he asked the feline, lifting him out of the contents. Napoleon gave a small "meow" as a response and stared morosely at his owner. Zenoni had trouble believing that the animal he rescued as a tiny stray while working the streets of Queens years before had turned into the seventeen-pound hyperactive creature he currently held.

"He got into the catnip earlier so he's acting out a little," Lorraine explained from where she sat, sticking red and green candles into a golden holder.

"How'd he manage that?"

Lorraine shrugged. "I was on the phone with Denise and wasn't paying attention to what he was doing. He knows we keep it in the cabinet; the door was a little open and he just weaseled his way in."

"How's Denise doing?"

"As well as she can, given the circumstances. Vincent's been home all day and he's being quiet—easy to handle for once. Denise doesn't know if he fully comprehends how much trouble he's in."

"He will soon enough," Zenoni reassured. "Believe me, the judge at his court case will hit everything right on home to him."

"How hard do you think they'll be on him?" Lorraine asked, concern lacing her words.

"I'd say no worse than community service."

"Think it'll work?"

"Hopefully. On my case today I spoke to someone who got into trouble as a juvenile for stealing and got community service at an animal shelter. He got really into dogs there and currently breeds them. From what I saw, he straightened himself out well. So, there's one success story."

"Provided he doesn't turn out to be the killer," Lorraine replied, smiling demurely.

"Right."

"I'm just praying Vincent behaves himself on Christmas day. We're going to have a full house and I don't want to deal with his attitude or antics—again."

Zenoni nodded. "I'm with you there. Remember last year when he took Adrianna and Brianna out for a spin in his car? I thought my sister was going to have a heart attack when she saw the way he drives."

"I still can't believe the girls came back laughing. I would have been scared half to death," Lorraine exclaimed.

"When I retire maybe we should just move into a senior citizen residence. No more decorations or family dinners or murder cases—that would be the life."

"You'd miss all this."

"At this point I wouldn't bet on it. The electric company surely would, though. Do you have any idea of how much extra this display adds to our bill?"

Lorraine rolled her eyes. "We built our lives around the holidays," she reminded. "Remember how we used to drive around various neighborhoods checking out how other people decorated?"

Zenoni smiled and nodded. His first date with Lorraine had consisted of driving aimlessly around different parts of Brooklyn to decide who had the most outlandish seasonal décor. Since then, the outing had become a tradition for the week prior to Christmas. Zenoni only hoped he would have his case solved by that time to ensure the tradition would be kept up this year too.

Incredibly, the day went quickly and by ten o'clock P.M., the Zenonis were hanging ornaments on the completed Christmas tree's branches as Napoleon rolled hyperly under the skirt of the tree. From the radio, Frank Sinatra was singing about "Chestnuts Roasting on an Open Fire." Lorraine was happily reminiscing about the origin of each ornament, clearly relieved that the decorating was finally coming together.

Not such a bad way to spend a Saturday, Zenoni thought, realizing that despite all his bellyaching and procrastinating, he really was enjoying the holiday season.

Chapter Nineteen

Distantly Zenoni heard the phone ringing. With an abundance of pure self-will, he opened his eyes and sat up in bed just enough to gaze at the bedside clock. It was 5:47 A.M. No one called this early on a Sunday morning unless it was important business—like police business. Nolan was on the other end of the line sounding absolutely exuberant and fully awake despite the early hour.

"There's been a major breakthrough in the case!" he exclaimed, practically stuttering with excitement. "I just heard from Sergeant Veglak that Hector Harte's woman, Margaret Bethany Scott, walked into a police station near her home at three in the morning and reported him for stealing and, she suspects, murder!"

"You're kidding me," Zenoni said. He was suddenly fully awake and his heart was pumping with adrenaline.

"I'm dead serious," Nolan replied. "The story is that a couple of hours after we left yesterday, Margaret got home and resumed her fighting with Hector. He got fed up and left the house in the truck. Margaret called her sister, who came and picked her up. Then the two of them started patrolling the neighborhood looking for Hector, who, she said, she still had 'a big bone to pick with.' Eventually, the two of them found him in a bar flirting with a waitress. Margaret lost her temper and decided to get even. She ended up walking into her local police station and told the officer on duty that Hector has been stealing jewelry from his workplace for years. She said he sold some pieces and gave others to her—although she swears she didn't know they were stolen until this afternoon when we made her suspicious. She even brought a whole bunch of gems with her to prove her point. Anyway, she said she thinks Hector might have killed Tiffany if she caught him stealing. She mentioned us by name too; she said we need to question Hector about his role in this."

"Do we know his whereabouts?"

"Local police picked him up and brought him over to our station."

"Is he fit to be interviewed?"

"He's got a few drinks in him, but he's fit to be questioned all right."

"I'm on my way," Zenoni told him, quickly removing himself from the bed. His fast-paced rummaging through drawers for his clothing woke Lorraine.

"What's going on?" she asked sleepily. Normally she could slumber through anything.

"I got a call," Zenoni replied, as he pulled a sock over his right foot. "I think my case just broke wide open. There's a suspect waiting for me down at the station."

"It isn't the community service guy, is it?" Lorraine asked with a slight smile, recalling their conversation the evening before.

"No, that was the security guard. We've got the janitor now. If this works out, I'll have this solved and, hopefully, have an extra week off for the Christmas holiday."

"And then just pray there's no more murders," Lorraine replied, already falling back into a deep sleep. "Be careful," she managed to groggily remark.

Zenoni slipped on his shoes and leaned down to kiss his

wife. "I will be," he promised, before running downstairs and grabbing both his coat and his car keys.

This is it, he thought, as he accelerated out of his driveway slightly faster than he should have. His gut told him that Tiffany's killer would be under arrest by the end of the day, and Angelo Zenoni's gut feelings were rarely wrong.

Chapter Twenty

Hector Harte's usual cocky, devil-may-care attitude had vanished. In its place was a stone-cold fear that had nestled itself deeply into the janitor's face. He sat inside Interview Room One twiddling his fingers and staring down at the floor. Angelo Zenoni and Nolan Wildow sat on the other side of the table preparing their notepads and giving the janitor occasional tough glances. It was 6:17 A.M.

"It seems like you've gotten yourself in a mess, Mr. Harte," Wildow suddenly announced, breaking the silence in the room.

Hector did not respond or raise his eyes.

"Do you care to tell us about the gemstones you stole or what you know about Tiffany's death?"

"Why do we go out getting ourselves all wound up about women?" Hector spat at the detectives, ignoring their questions.

"Well, you know how it is," Wildow replied matter-of-factly. "You can't live with them and you can't live without them."

"She's ruined my life!" Hector exclaimed, sounding like he was on the verge of tears. "She's really gone and done it this time!"

"The evidence does put you in a pretty bad light," Zenoni admitted, "but you can help yourself if you tell us the truth right now and up front. We know you stole, but prove to us that you're innocent of any other crimes. Come right out and tell us what happened. Be honest, show us you have nothing to hide, and it will make your time in court a whole lot easier."

Hector looked up and faced the detectives for the first time since being brought into the interview room. Zenoni could clearly see stress and fear in the man's eyes.

"Okay, I admit it. I stole from the studio," the janitor confessed.

"How much?" Wildow demanded.

"I don't even know. It's been going on for years. Me and Nelson, the night guard, are in it together. He shuts off the cameras just long enough so I can grab the gems."

"And no one noticed?"

"It was late at night and the studio's always a mess anyway. Genson can't manage nothing right. He doesn't have any idea what's coming in or going out of the studio. He doesn't even have the shipping order dates down right. Nine times out of ten, he's surprised when the truck arrives with new stuff. It ain't too hard for stuff to go missing in that whole mess and I'm not stupid. I take a few gems at a time from different crates. It's subtle, you know what I mean?"

"How about Tiffany?" Zenoni asked. "Did she notice?"

Hector nodded. "Yeah, man. That was the whole problem. She was the one person who actually paid attention when stuff disappeared. I used to have to sneak around her, dodging questions and mean looks. She knew I was up to something. I don't know how she knew, but she did. I don't think she had any real proof, though, or I'd have been in trouble way sooner than this. Who woulda thought my own woman would be the one to blow the whistle on me? Especially after I gave her all them nice gifts too!"

"How about the night of the murder?" Wildow interrupted. "Were you stealing that night?"

Hector nodded.

"Did Tiffany see you taking something?"

Hector vigorously shook his head. "I was careful around her. I always watched my step. She used to watch me on the sly. She didn't want to let me know she was watching, but I knew. I'm not stupid enough to think she wasn't suspicious."

"What time was it?"

"About quarter past two in the morning. Everyone was supposed to be at home by then, but Tiffany never left. She was always there, prowling around. I only took half a case worth of stuff. I needed to sneak it out without her noticing and that was much easier said than done."

Zenoni leaned forward in his chair and stared intently at the nervous janitor. "Here's where I have trouble believing you," he declared. "You see, I think Tiffany saw you and threatened to report you. I think you lost your temper and tried to prevent her from making a complaint. I'm sure you didn't mean to kill her, but it sure seems like something went wrong."

"That's not true!" Hector cried, truly panicked for the first time in the investigation. "Look, I was working serious overtime. I never hang around there *that* late unless I have to! As soon as I realized she was sniffing around, I played it real cool and clocked out as soon as I could."

"Were the cameras on or off when you left?" Wildow asked.

"They were supposed to be put back on to avoid suspicion, but Nelson is a grade-A idiot and he forgot. I think he was sleeping; it's all the guy does."

Zenoni nodded. *That explains why they were still off when we arrived,* he thought.

"So when was the last time you saw Tiffany?" he pressed.

"A few minutes before I left. She was in the back room rummaging through inventory papers. She was obsessed with knowing exactly what she'd be showing ahead of time, so she could get sales pitch ideas or something like that."

"And she said nothing to you?"

"Not a word."

"What happened when you got out of the studio?" Wildow asked, staring hard at his suspect.

"I went back to my truck," Hector mumbled.

"Where was it parked?"

"In the back lot."

"So you went out the back door, right past Tiffany?"

Hector nodded.

"Okay. What happened when you got into your truck? Did you go straight home?"

Hector did not reply. He simply put his head in his hands and sighed deeply.

"Being truthful with us is the only way to really help yourself," Zenoni explained while tapping his pen monotonously on the tabletop. "Honestly, this story you're telling sounds pretty weak, and given what you've said about the time you were at the location and the presence of the victim, I'd say we have enough to hold you as a suspect. Unless, of course, you give us something substantial in the next few minutes that will help get the spotlight off your involvement in all this."

"Okay, fine," Hector cried, dropping his hands and exposing his tormented face. "I left soon after getting in my truck, but not right away. I was happy about getting out of there without a hassle and it was real late, and I was tired and I decided I deserved a little reward. I had me a little celebration whiskey—not a lot, just what I carry in my flask."

"And for how long do you think you drank?"

"I told you already, not much. I got home all right, didn't I?"

"I meant in the sense of time. How long were you sitting there drinking?"

"Not long. Fifteen minutes maybe."

"And that's it?"

"Yeah, but I saw something weird."

"And what was that?"

"I didn't wanna say anything knowing how you guys feel about folks who drive after having a few drinks, but. I'm screwed now anyway, so what does it matter? I'll tell you. As I was sitting in the truck, I heard an engine roaring and tires squealing. I looked out my window just in time to see this van driving up to the studio real erratically. It stopped right by the building and someone jumped out of the driver's side—I think there was only one person in the van—and ran into the back door of the studio. I guess the door was unlocked; they didn't look like they were struggling with a key."

"Was this person male or female?"

"I don't know. I couldn't see. It was dark and I was *a little* drunk."

"Did you get the license plate number?"

"No. I never thought of checking that out. I figured that whatever was going on had nothing to do with me and I should keep to my own business."

"Can you describe the van?"

Hector nodded. "Yeah, it was old. It looked like a late 1980s or early 1990s model. It was red, but not bright—dark and kinda murky, almost brownish. Then again, the yellow parking lot lights probably made it seem worse than it was. But there was enough light for me to notice that the back bumper was broken, all smashed in, as if someone had hit it a while back. And that's it, I swear—that's all I know! After the driver jumped out and ran into the studio, I just drove away. I didn't want to be seen with the stolen stuff. Oh Lord, I've done myself in this time!"

Wailing, Hector put his head back in his hands and rested on the table as he babbled about the misfortunes of his life. Zenoni and Wildow simply stared at one another. They knew the vehicle Hector was talking about. It was the van that belonged to Tiffany's downstairs neighbor, Blanche Jiranek.

Chapter Twenty-one

A half hour later, Hector was under arrest and being processed at the station. Zenoni and Wildow had already left headquarters and were driving to Blanche's house. It was a bitterly cold morning, despite the cloudless blue sky, and Zenoni thanked God for small favors, like the working heater in his vehicle. Traffic was practically nonexistent, enabling him to drive at a steady sixty-five miles an hour. He left his sirens and lights off. He didn't want to attract attention.

It was 7:03 in the morning and the suburban streets were still awakening. On weekdays, men and women would be heading off to work, but on this quiet weekend morning the streets were still. Zenoni saw two women in robes collecting the morning paper from their doorsteps. In a few front yards, dogs ran around barking behind picket fences. Other than that, the suburb could have been a ghost town.

Tiffany's apartment complex resembled a huge dollhouse in the morning light. Seven A.M. appeared to be too early for the residents of Maple Cove Condominiums—not a single soul was spotted walking around the premises. The only signs of life were the birds tweeting away in the bare branches of the surrounding foliage. As Zenoni parked his car, he wondered at the paradox of how an area as seemingly peaceful as Long Island could also be the same place in which a murder like Tiffany's was committed.

Blanche's van was parked outside her apartment; the sight of it filled Zenoni with anticipation. Perhaps he would have this case solved sooner than expected. He and Wildow strolled up to the door and rang the bell. The sudden sound of the buzzer apparently surprised Blanche and led to quite a commotion behind the closed door. Nearly a minute passed before Blanche answered, looking tired and disheveled. She had obviously been interrupted in the middle of dressing for work. She wore a light blue shirt and skirt; the white apron that came with the outfit was clenched tightly in her left hand. Her makeup was only half applied and her hair was set in curlers. She wore no shoes. Behind her, a small bespectacled boy sat in front of a television watching cartoons.

"What do you want?" Blanche demanded, immediately recognizing the detectives and clearly peeved by their presence.

"Mrs. Jiranek, we need to speak with you," Wildow announced.

"You're kidding, right?" she snapped. "Can't you see how busy I am right now? I have to be at work by seven thirty sharp or my boss will make it a personal mission to belittle me in front of all the other waitresses, most of whom are airhead dropouts or poor pensioners trying to earn a little extra on the side. And trust me, they all like to gossip behind my back! I don't need to deal with that this morning, and I certainly don't need to deal with you!"

With that said, Blanche tried to slam the door in the detectives' faces, but Zenoni put his foot inside the doorway to prevent it from closing. The ache in his toes from the pressure was almost excruciating, yet he did not allow a trace of discomfort to show on his face. "I'm afraid we need to speak with you *now*," he insisted solemnly. "It's urgent."

Blanche's eyes were fiery with rage and disbelief. "What is wrong with you? Can't you see that I'm getting dressed? I don't have time to stand around and answer questions. I already told you I need to get to work." Once again she tried to close the door, unsuccessfully due to Zenoni's resistance.

"Ma'am, we are conducting a murder investigation and we *must* speak with you. Work is not your top priority right now. I suggest you call your boss and tell him you'll be late or not there at all today. One way or another you're coming with us first."

"What do you mean coming with you?" she shrieked.

"We have reason to conduct this as a formal interrogation in an interview room. You need to be at the police station for that to happen."

"This must be a joke," Blanche exclaimed, sounding nervous for the first time. "You can't do this. This can't happen!"

"I'm afraid it can and it will," Wildow replied, edging up to the door.

"What about Lawrence?" Blanche asked, pointing to the small boy watching television. "I have nowhere to leave my son. He's got an ear infection, so he's out of school."

"In that case he can come with you," Zenoni replied. "May we come in? We'll give you a few minutes to get yourself together before we head out."

Blanche fixed the detectives with an ice-cold stare before unwillingly moving aside and allowing them entry into her home.

"No snooping!" she snapped. "You really have no idea how much this messes my day up! Just don't touch anything. I'll be out in a few minutes."

As soon as the lawmen had stepped into the foyer, Blanche slammed the door and proceeded to march into her bedroom and vanish behind the door. Zenoni took a moment to survey the apartment. It was such a far cry from Tiffany's life of semi-luxury that it was hard to believe a single floor was all that separated the two households. Blanche's home was cluttered with cheap furniture. Discarded pieces of clothing were strewn around the worn carpet, which looked as if it had not been vacuumed since the New Year. The blinds were drawn over the windows with dust clinging to them visibly. Stuffing peeked through holes in the tattered couch. Zenoni peered into the kitchen and saw dirty dishes and cups piled high in the sink; the refrigerator hummed loudly as if protesting the mess.

Zenoni then turned his attention to the small boy sitting in front of the television. He gave the detectives a brief glance and then turned back to the program, seemingly uninterested in the presence of the two men. Close up, the boy was even paler and skinnier than Zenoni remembered. It was obvious that he had a considerable number of health problems, and Zenoni suddenly found himself feeling a deep sense of sympathy for Blanche. *It can't be easy dealing with this alone,* he thought. *No wonder she's so edgy.* As soon as the thought crossed his mind, Blanche hurried out of her bedroom, fiddling with her purse and coat while looking tenser than ever.

"Okay, let's get this over with. I want to be back on track as soon as possible without any more of these rude little interruptions." She was staring hatefully at the detectives as she spoke, but the hardness in her face didn't hide the tremble in her hands. "Lawrence!" she shrieked, directing her attention to the boy. "Turn that thing off! How many times have I told you not to sit so close to it? And use a chair! You'll strain your back sitting on the floor like that! I mean it; turn the television off right now. Mommy has to go talk with these men and you have to come with her."

"But I'm watching cartoons!" the boy protested, unfazed by the nagging. For the first time Blanche looked at the screen and noticed that *The Simpsons* were on. Scowling, she marched over to the television and switched it off, much to her son's dismay.

"I had PBS on and I told you not to change the channel!" she scolded. "Cartoons lower your IQ, and that's an adult cartoon; you shouldn't be watching it anyway."

"I was looking for *Scooby Doo*."

"*Scooby Doo* isn't on channel five."

"Doctor Hutchenson lets me watch *Scooby Doo*."

"That's because Dr. Hutchenson has cable in her office. Cable is too expensive for us!" Blanche snapped, as she lifted her whining son into her arms and made her way toward the front door. Zenoni walked ahead of her and held it open.

"I don't need your assistance!" Blanche snapped angrily, as she walked out the door. Zenoni simply smiled and shrugged, refusing to let her rudeness bother him.

After locking the door, Blanche walked toward her car. Lawrence, holstered in her arms, was still complaining about his inability to watch his favorite cartoon.

"Mrs. Jiranek, we're going to have to insist you come in our car," Wildow announced.

"Oh I know that!" Blanche retorted angrily. "I'm not a total idiot! My son needs his blanket; he gets cold easily. I left it in the backseat."

Zenoni looked over at Wildow and shrugged. Lawrence did seem like the sort of kid who would be prone to pretty much every cold out there. After securing her son's blue-and-white-striped blanket, Blanche entered the police car without incident. The drive back to the station was uneventful, except for the relentless interest Lawrence showed in his surroundings. Upon being let out of the house, Lawrence had come alive. Awed by being in a police car, he was determined to conduct a never-ending interrogation about everything police-related.

"Why don't you turn on your sirens and lights like the police in the movies do?" he asked.

"Because we aren't in a big rush," Zenoni explained.

"Oh. I like the sirens and lights. The ambulances at the hospital have them on sometimes."

"That makes sense," Zenoni replied pleasantly; he had to admit that the kid was kind of cute.

"Do you arrest a lot of bad guys?"

"We do our best."

"Do you put the handcuffs on them?"

"Sure do."

"How many bad guys do you arrest in a day? Twenty? Thirty? A hundred?"

Zenoni chuckled. "Not that many, kid. The neighborhood isn't that tough."

The detective's responses seemed to invigorate Lawrence and launch him into a tide of questions: "What's the baddest neighborhood you were ever in? Who's the baddest person you ever saw? Did you ever shoot anyone? Have you been shot? Did anyone ever get away from you? Did you ever have to chase somebody in a car or a boat or a helicopter? Did—"

"Lawrence, be quiet!" Blanche suddenly shouted. "Don't overexcite yourself!"

"I'm not overexcited!"

"You're being annoying, and Mommy has a migraine. I don't need any more aggravation!"

"What's aggravation mean?"

"It means you're frustrating me!"

"What's frustrating mean?

"Lawrence, shut your mouth!"

Although the exchange had left Zenoni biting the insides of his cheeks to avoid laughter, he became more solemn when he looked in the rearview mirror. Blanche was gazing out the window, appearing near to tears. Lawrence was wrapped tightly in the cocoon of his blanket, staring silently out the opposite side window. Zenoni felt a deep pang of pity for the boy. Obviously the hard conditions of her life had affected Blanche's attitude toward her own son.

The remainder of the car ride was spent in silence, but Lawrence perked right up and started asking questions again the moment he realized he was at a real police station. He wanted to know how old the station was, how many cells it had, and how many bad guys had gotten "pinched" there each year. Lawrence hurried excitedly into the station, as Blanche, flanked by the detectives, followed him, fixedly staring down at the ground. Lawrence was drawn to the fish tank the moment he entered. Sandra distracted the boy with feeding the fish as Zenoni and Wildow led Blanche into Interview Room One.

Despite her initial hostility, Blanche sat compliantly with her hands folded atop the table. Zenoni was anticipating talking to her, but as usual before interviews, there was a pit of anxiety in his stomach. If Blanche refused to speak with them and instead opted to contact a lawyer, there was little they could do to uncover the true motive behind the murder.

Wildow switched on the recorder and noted the time and date of the interview aloud. Blanche watched this procedure in silence. "I suppose you know why you're here, Mrs. Jiranek," he then said, addressing his suspect for the first time.

"Not really," Blanche snapped. "I suspect it has something to do with my murdered neighbor, but I already told you that wasn't my fault."

"We have some information that contradicts that statement," Zenoni replied.

Blanche diverted her eyes, but her expression remained stony. "Whatever you heard is wrong."

"Why don't you tell us a little bit about your relationship with Tiffany?"

This request caused Blanche to rear up her head in anger. "We didn't have any relationship! She was just a neighbor, and a bad one at that! She had absolutely no regard for anyone but herself. I had nothing at all to do with her aside from being unfortunate enough to live downstairs from her, and I never had any desire to get to know her better."

"Did you quarrel often?"

"She was noisy! I complained a few times because it was a violation of my quality of life. Other than that, no, we didn't quarrel."

"How did she handle your complaining?"

Blanche snorted back laughter. "She couldn't have cared less. She paid no attention at all; she thought she was above everyone."

"You sound tense even talking about her," Wildow observed.

"Of course I'm tense!" Blanche screeched. "I should be at work right now and instead I'm sitting here discussing the murder of a neighbor I hardly knew! Is that stressful enough for you, because I could go on! I work seven days a week as a waitress, constantly getting harassed by the world's most annoying people for minimum wage! Every second of spare time I get is spent getting my son medical care. He's frail. You wouldn't even believe the health problems he's got: asthma, hearing impairment, poor vision, and more allergies than you can imagine. He's allergic to the sun, for God's sake! So, yes, I'm tense. What mother wouldn't be after all that? And I do it all on my own!"

"So let's make that clear," Zenoni retorted, slightly taken aback by Blanche's sudden rant. "You live with your son and no one else? Is that correct?"

"Yes," Blanche declared, instantly launching into another

tirade. "And don't look at me like that! I know what you're thinking: 'Lawrence has no father.' Well, let me tell you right now that you're wrong! I was married for three years before I had Lawrence. Spencer, his father, left right after he was born. He couldn't accept the health problems our son had. We used to be big into the party scene and he said I had messed up my body and made Lawrence the way he is. Some father, right? He even went as far as saying that Lawrence wasn't his son. When he left, I didn't miss him. I only keep the name Jiranek—that's Spencer's last name, mine is Wilmot—for Lawrence. It just seemed better, more proper, for us to have the same last name in this increasingly judgmental society."

Zenoni put his hand up to cut off Blanche's word flow. "Mrs. Jiranek—"

"I just said *my* name's Wilmot!"

"Fine then, Miss Wilmot, please, just answer my question simply: Is there anyone else who is either living with you, or not living with you, who might have access to your car?"

"No! I already told you that Spencer's been gone for years. We never formally divorced, but of course he's got himself some illegitimate replacement children living two towns over with this blond fool who—"

"Aside from Spencer," Zenoni cut in, raising his voice in annoyance, "might anyone else have access to your van?"

Blanche was outraged. "Are you implying that I'm some kind of Jezebel who has many men in her house who she also lends her car to?"

"NO!" Zenoni shouted. His head was spinning. "Mrs. Jiranek—Wilmot! I meant Miss Wilmot. I am just trying to establish that, aside from you, no one else would be likely to drive your van?"

"Not unless a thief took it, and I'm not lucky enough for that, because that means I could get an insurance claim."

"Well, that puts us in a bit of a pickle," Wildow exclaimed, mercifully giving Zenoni time to rest his vocal cords. "We've got a witness telling us that a vehicle matching your van's description, right down to the broken bumper, was seen speeding into the studio's back parking lot mere minutes before Tiffany was murdered. Furthermore, our witness tells us that a figure jumped out of the parked van and ran into the unlocked back door of the studio. That's the exact location where Tiffany's lifeless body was discovered a few hours later. Do you care to explain that?"

All the color drained from Blanche's face; she looked as pale as Casper the Friendly Ghost. "No, I think you must be mistaken. I was home with my son the night Tiffany died. At that hour, I was fast asleep, and I can assure you that I don't drive when I'm sleeping."

Zenoni leaned forward and placed his elbows firmly on the table, making sure to stare at Blanche as sternly as possible. "I don't believe you. I think you're hiding something from me. I can see it on your face. I'm going to find out what you're hiding no matter how long I have to keep this interview up. If this does end up in court, however, it will be in your best interest to confess right now. It will cast you in a better light for the jury."

"That's too bad, because I have nothing to say to any jury or to you. I was home sleeping the night Tiffany died."

"We all make mistakes sometimes," Zenoni replied, trying the soothing approach. "And keeping things on our conscience can turn into a real hassle after some time. Miss Wilmot, if you have something to tell us, I suggest you do so now. Nothing is insurmountable. If you're honest with us about why your van was in the lot right before the murder, I think we'll all be a lot happier."

"I have nothing to tell," Blanche insisted. "I didn't do anything wrong."

"The problem with that story is we all know it's not true!" Zenoni shouted, reaching the end of his rope. "We have a witness who identified your van to a tee, and this is someone who isn't likely to have seen it before. I think you're lying to me, and I don't like it one little bit."

"I was at home sleeping," Blanche declared, through clenched teeth.

"All right," Zenoni retorted, straining to control his temper amid his increasing frustration. "You're really going to tell me that you weren't at the studio on the night Tiffany was murdered?"

"No, I was not," Blanche persisted, staring down at the tabletop.

"And you have nothing at all to get off your conscience?"

"No."

"So, you're just going to sit here and lie to us with absolutely no regard for the family of that poor woman?"

"Tiffany Kehl was anything but a poor woman!" Blanche screamed, losing all sense of composure as she raised her eyes from the table and glared at Zenoni. "She was the worst sort of witch I ever met! You can't even begin to imagine what it was like living with her as a neighbor! And it wasn't just her pounding around her hardwood floor in high heels during the wee hours of the morning—mostly it was that stupid little dog of hers! It never ever stops barking! I thought it would drive me insane. I complained to Tiffany, but she just laughed it off or told me to stop being so dramatic. Then she'd ignore me, and of course that useless landlord never listened either. He was too preoccupied by whatever tight, low-cut top Tiffany had on that day to pay any mind to my problems! I was tormented by that evil witch! She was *anything* but a poor woman!" Blanche was practically snarling. The color was high in her cheeks, and her eyes were alive with rage as she stared down the detectives.

She's a ticking time bomb, Zenoni realized. He had been on the police force for a long time and he knew a mentally unstable person when he saw one. Blanche had been provoked into a tantrum, and Zenoni knew that if he played his cards just right, he would be able to get her to confess.

"Blanche, did you go to the studio that night to confront Tiffany?" he asked, placing his hand on her arm in what he hoped was a supportive manner. At first she was unresponsive and then, suddenly and unexpectantly, Blanche's eyes filled with tears.

"I couldn't take it anymore," she sobbed. "The horrible little creature never stopped yapping and no one would do anything to help me stop it! No one cared that it was ruining my life. I couldn't sleep because of it and my energy level at work was zapped, which caused even more tension on my job. And then there was Lawrence. He couldn't sleep either because of that dog! This has been going on since I moved in two years ago!"

"What happened on Monday night leading into Tuesday morning?" Zenoni asked gently, as Blanche tried to stop her sobs. Wordlessly, Wildow handed her a tissue, which she accepted and used to blow her nose.

"I had a bad day. I woke up late to the sound of that *thing* upstairs barking itself hoarse. I was late getting into work and the manager was yelling at me. His mood wasn't improved when he saw Lawrence was with me; I had nowhere else to put him. I worked a double shift, and by the time I got home, I was coughing. I think I picked up a sore throat from Lawrence; he's prone to strep. Things got worse when I walked into my apartment and discovered that a pipe in the wall had burst and left a huge brown wet stain on my living room wall! Then, right as we were about to go to sleep, that animal upstairs started to howl. I couldn't sleep and neither could my son. I walked upstairs and banged on the door, but Tiffany wasn't home. I tried the landlord's office, but they weren't around either, and I wasn't going to call the police over a barking dog. So, I went back to my place and gave Lawrence some sleeping pills. I know it was a little risky, but his system is used to medication and he needed to rest. As soon as he was deeply asleep, I went out.

"I knew where Tiffany worked—I had seen her on TV once when I was flipping channels at Lawrence's doctor's office— and I had a pretty good idea of where the studio was located. I was furious, but I just wanted to talk to her, to give her a piece of my mind and tell her off once and for all. I found the sign for the studio and drove around the building until I spotted her car parked in the back lot. I pulled in, parked, and ran into the building through the back door. Tiffany was standing right there, holding a tray of gems. She looked totally taken by surprise to see me there, and before she could say anything to me, I started yelling at her about her dog. And do you know what she said to me? Do you?"

Blanche was leaning forward in her chair. Her eyes were wide and somehow lost in their own realm. Her lips quivered with anger.

Never removing his eyes from hers, Zenoni shook his head. "No, Blanche, I don't know. Please tell me what Tiffany said to you."

"She told me she was working and too busy to deal with my hysterics—those were her exact words! She just brushed me off and told me I had no right to be at her job. She told me she was going to call the police if I didn't leave. I lost my temper and told her the dog was driving me crazy. I demanded she get rid of it. She told me to move, as if finding another house was simple, and then she turned her back to me! All the while she was telling me to go home, and to stop and buy earplugs on the way! I just lost control. As soon as her back was turned, I grabbed the thing closest to me—I think it was a lamp—and I swung it as hard as I could at her. The lamp hit her right on the back of the head. I heard a *crack* and saw blood, and then she just fell on the floor and didn't move again. I think I might have hit her a few more times after that, but I'm not sure. I just remember staring at her lying there, and then thanking God it was cold and I'd worn my gloves, so there would be no fingerprints.

"I thought I was going to be caught right away—we had made enough noise during the exchange—but no one came. I just dropped the lamp and went home. I put the clothes I'd been wearing in a garbage bag and threw them out. Then I went to bed. I thought if I just went about my normal business, I'd go under the radar of the ensuing investigation. But then, right before I went to sleep, I was hit with the crippling fear that the security cameras had got me on tape and the police would be surrounding my house any second. Then I remembered all the times I'd heard Tiffany screaming on her phone at that Arnold guy about how the cameras never worked, so I hoped I had gotten away lucky. I tried to carry on normally, but I've lived every second since that night in fear! Every time the door to the diner opened, I jumped a mile thinking the police were closing in. I haven't slept in days. I can't eat. And it's all for nothing—you've got me anyway, because of some random witness I didn't even see! The worst part is I'm relieved! Everything is falling apart, and I just want it all to stop and go away. I didn't mean to kill her. I honestly didn't plan to!"

Realizing that she had just cracked and confessed to killing Tiffany over the barking of a dog, Blanche dissolved into tears. Zenoni sat silently in his seat and watched Blanche in shock. It was rare to get such a detailed and emotion-filled confession. After six days, his case was solved, but his heart was too heavy with the facts to be happy about the outcome. A young woman had been murdered by a stressed and overworked single mother because of a barking dog—and a sickly seven-year-old boy was trapped in the middle of the mess. Zenoni wished that he had the power to turn back time and prevent the crime, but being merely mortal, all he could do was see to it that Blanche could never again launch into a murderous rage on an unsuspecting victim.

Half an hour later Blanche had been formally arrested. The police were in the process of contacting Spencer, Lawrence's estranged father, to come claim his son. Lawrence was blissfully unaware of what was happening; the detectives had made sure to shield the child from the sight of his mother being led away in handcuffs. Currently Lawrence was sitting happily in front of the office TV watching *Tom and Jerry* cartoons. Someone, most likely Sandra, had supplied him with a soft drink and a chocolate bar from the vending machine. Twice he asked why his mother was gone for so long, but mostly he was too preoccupied by the TV show to inquire.

"Some turnout, huh?" Wildow asked, joining Zenoni in the hallway, where he stood eyeing Lawrence pitifully from a distance.

"Sure is. So close to Christmas too."

"It's a sad one, all right. I just hope the father comes for that kid. He's been through enough already."

Zenoni nodded. "I'm with you there. I can't imagine a fragile kid like him in foster care."

"Well, at least we got our killer," Wildow declared heartily, giving Zenoni a congratulatory pat on the back.

"That's true," Zenoni admitted. Even though his heart ached for the son of the murderer, he was pleased that he had successfully managed to get justice for Tiffany Kehl.

Chapter Twenty-two

It had been a week since the confession and subsequent arrest of Blanche Jiranek. The story of Tiffany Kehl's murder was all over the news, alongside praise for Angelo Zenoni and Nolan Wildow, who were getting letters of thanks from the very politicians who had previously scrutinized their handling of the case.

Blanche Wilmot Jiranek had been charged with second-degree murder and was awaiting trial. Lawrence's father—who had come to collect his son about two hours after the arrest—was attempting to gain legal custody of the boy.

Alex Dedek was sentenced to therapy sessions and community service, plus a hefty two-thousand-dollar fine for his part in resisting arrest and obstructing the course of justice during a murder investigation. His lawyer was attempting to appeal the case on the grounds that his client had been insane with grief upon hearing of his love interest's death, but Zenoni was fairly certain that Alex's sentence would not be changed.

Both Hector Harte, the television studio janitor, and Nelson Rosley, the night shift security guard, had been arrested for theft and were awaiting trial. Amazingly, Margaret Bethany Scott, the same woman who had gotten Hector arrested, was standing by her man while he sat in prison. Apparently pleased that he was not under suspicion for murder, Margaret claimed that Hector's imprisonment would be a good time to work on their relationship. After all, with him behind bars, there was no possible way another woman could come between them. For his part, Hector needed Margaret to visit him with cigarettes and magazines, and so despite everything, it looked as if their relationship was to remain in place.

After closing the case Nolan Wildow had taken an early vacation so he could help his wife rid the house of dust and germs before company arrived for Christmas. It might sound dull, Wildow had explained to Zenoni, but anything seemed pleasant after looking at dead bodies. When put in those terms, Zenoni had to agree with his partner.

In Zenoni's opinion, the best part of solving the case was finally having the time to finish his holiday decorations. Currently, he was perched atop his roof, nailing down a large plastic image of Santa in a sled led by twelve reindeer. Two stories below him, Lorraine, Denise, and Vincent were putting the final touches on the front lawn display, as Viviane, out of the senior center for the day, supervised from her seat on the front porch. Knowing that Zenoni had been behind in his decorating, Denise had decided that having Vincent help set up the ornaments was the perfect way to repay his uncle. Every now and then, Zenoni would glance down at his scowling nephew and smirk. The kid didn't look too happy about sticking Santa hats on animated figures, and the fact that Vincent looked annoyed and inconvenienced seemed like poetic justice to Zenoni. Yet, truth be told, Vincent did seem to be getting a bit more cooperative. Just that morning, Zenoni had suggested the kid take up a hobby, like charity work or sports, to keep him out of trouble, and for once, Vincent seemed somewhat interested in his uncle's suggestions.

It was chilly on the roof, but the air lacked the biting cold that had tormented Zenoni in years past, and the clear weather forecast for the rest of the day was something to be thankful for. As he worked, Zenoni's mind wandered to thoughts of the Kehls and little Lawrence; this would be a hard Christmas for them. Zenoni had not seen Lawrence since the day of his mother's arrest, but on the day Tiffany was buried at the Seminole Lane Cemetery, Zenoni had watched the ceremony from a distance. He did not want to intrude on the family in their time of grief, but he had been pleased to see Christie and Evelyn and Thomas Kehl standing close together peacefully, as they watched Tiffany's mahogany casket being lowered into the ground. Perhaps it was possible that being together for the funeral would reunite the estranged family.

Retirement was still looming in Zenoni's mind and growing greater with every passing day, but he didn't think he was ready to leave the force yet. Maybe just a few more cases . . .

"When you're finished with that, come in and have some hot chocolate—it's just made!" Lorraine suddenly called from the festive front lawn, jolting Zenoni out of his thoughts.

"Get back to work!" Zenoni joked.

"Can't," Lorraine retorted with a huge smile on her face. "Once you're finished up there, we're all set! All we gotta do then is enjoy the hot chocolate and wait for night to fall so we can light it all up!"

And so that night, amid his family and a handful of anticipating neighbors, Angelo switched his lights on and officially kicked off the Christmas season, Zenoni-style. As he stood on the street outside his home and watched the festive ornaments shine and sing, and blink and dance, he smiled. Despite the stress of the past week, he could not complain about his life. Wordlessly taking his wife's hand in his, Detective Angelo Zenoni anticipated a wonderful Christmas and a peaceful New Year.

WETUMPKA PUBLIC LIBRARY
212 SOUTH MAIN STREET
WETUMPKA, Al   36092